STABBED
IN THE
TART

STABBED IN THE TART

THE HSP MYSTERIES

CAROL E. AYER

CAMEL PRESS

Kenmore, WA

CAMEL PRESS

A Camel Press book published by Epicenter Press

Epicenter Press
6524 NE 181st St.
Suite 2
Kenmore, WA 98028

For more information go to:
www.Camelpress.com
www.Coffeetownpress.com
www.Epicenterpress.com
www. carolayer.com

Cover and interior design by Scott Book and Melissa Vail Coffman

Stabbed in the Tart
Copyright © 2021 by Carol E. Ayer

ISBN: 978-1-94207-820-3 (Trade Paper)
ISBN: 978-1-94207-821-0 (eBook)

Printed in the United States of America

To my mom, Penny Strohl.
Thank you for your never-ending support.
One day we'll get our beach house!

ACKNOWLEDGMENTS

I'd like to thank my agent, Dawn Dowdle of Blue Ridge Literary Agency. I can always count on Dawn to help me through the process of writing a book, promptly answering questions and lending a supportive ear. Jennifer McCord, my editor at Camel, is fabulous at determining what my books are lacking and leading the way to a better story. Thanks to Jennifer, Phil Garrett, cover/interior designers Scott Book and Melissa Vail Coffman, and everyone at Camel Press.

I would also like to thank Sarah Burr for reading an early version of the manuscript and for giving me top-rate suggestions for how to improve it. Sarah is a wonderful beta reader and a terrific writer.

I based the fictional Countryside Inn loosely on The Inn at Death Valley, a place I've never visited but would love to stay in one day! The fictional Playworld is based on the defunct amusement parks Playland and Neptune Beach, which were popular attractions in the San Francisco Bay Area in the twentieth century.

CHAPTER 1

I PEERED THROUGH THE WINDSHIELD, reimagining the math problems I'd enjoyed solving in high school: If a car traveling at the rate of one mile per hour is headed toward a hotel five miles away where the driver is due in ten minutes, what is the likelihood of the vehicle arriving on time? If the car does *not* arrive on time, what is the probability of the driver getting in big trouble?

The answers were clear. I would be late and in big trouble.

The traffic had been bumper-to-bumper from the moment I'd left Oceanville on the central California coast headed thirty miles to the east. The unseasonably warm and blustery February day wasn't making anything easier. In an attempt to cool myself down, I'd rolled down my windows, but the wind had done a number on my hair. I would have to attend to it as soon as I got to the hotel and be delayed even further.

The cars in front of me slowed to a dead stop. I revised my first math problem to a car traveling at the rate of zero miles per hour. The probability of the driver being in big trouble rose accordingly.

As I stared out the window at the strip mall to my left, hoping against hope that the car ahead of me would eventually inch forward, I reviewed how I had gotten myself into this situation.

Three days earlier, Amanda Longfellow, a baker I'd met at an expo in Los Angeles in December, had called to plead with me to take over her role of guest dessert chef at The Countryside Inn located in Los Robles, the original seat of Ocean County. After a moment of thinking it over and deciding the gig could be good for my business, Kayla's Home-Baked Goods by the Sea, I'd agreed. The following day, the hotel owner and kitchen manager cleared me to fill in and my weekend was set.

Curious about the place where I'd be spending my long Valentine's weekend, I'd done some research. The historic hotel was built in the 1920s and had survived two earthquakes, a fire, and, in later years, near bankruptcy. In its heyday, Hollywood stars, politicians, journalists, and authors had been esteemed guests. It remained a playground for the rich and famous for many decades.

By the dawn of the twenty-first century, the hotel was showing its age and no longer attracting its usual celebrated clientele. The Countryside managed to hold on by a thread until 2015, when tech billionaire Conrad Cunningham purchased the grand hotel for a mind-blowing amount of money and refurbished it to its former glory—with modern conveniences, of course. By 2018, The Countryside was flourishing as one of the county's must-sees for tourists. Young celebrity sightings had added to its cachet.

Guest chef weekends, a recent addition to the hotel's offerings, were cleverly titled "Gourmet and Stay" and included several lunches and dinners as part of the special rate. Well-known chefs such as Katie McClure, Isaac Norland, and Diane Bayumi had all made appearances. I wasn't sure how my desserts would stack up against such brilliance, but I would give it my best try.

The traffic finally picked up. I entered Los Robles city limits and found the street that led to The Countryside, a lonely and dusty old road populated only by a plethora of oak trees. The street clearly hadn't been updated with the rest of the hotel. I followed the road to the end, located a space in the crowded parking lot, and grabbed my messenger bag from the passenger seat. I didn't have luggage since I was going to commute from Oceanville for the three-day event. My cat, Flour, had a watery eye, and I was watching her closely in case a vet visit was indicated.

As I walked toward the front entrance, glancing over to where I'd read tennis courts and a glamorous outdoor pool once stood, a strong wind gust caused me to lose my balance. I stopped to regain my equilibrium and gazed up at my destination.

The hotel was both charming and imposing. Inspired by Spanish missions, the building boasted a red tiled roof, arched doorways and windows, and stucco walls. It was really quite beautiful.

I went inside, worrying over how late I was. I would have to leave earlier on Sunday and Monday to ensure I arrived in plenty of time for lunch service.

The lobby offered several chairs and couches for sitting and featured an art deco ceiling. Classical music played over the sound system, giving me a brief respite from my stress. I saw a restroom off the lobby but decided to wait to deal with my hair. I couldn't afford to be any later than I already was.

I asked at the front desk for Conrad Cunningham. The clerk pointed to her left to the restaurant and I went in, taking note of the red tablecloths and the crystal vases overflowing with pink roses. In a few hours, hotel guests would sit at these very tables and eat one of my desserts at the end of their meals. A little quiver of excitement ran through me.

"Kayla Jeffries?" a voice said.

I turned to see a trim man wearing dress pants and a black blazer walking toward me, hand extended. I recognized Conrad Cunningham immediately from photos and news reports I'd seen over the years.

"Yes, I'm Kayla."

"Conrad Cunningham." I knew Conrad had recently turned sixty-five, thirty years older than myself. His dark hair was streaked with grey, and his brown eyes looked tired. He wasn't classically handsome, but he had a certain presence that I found a tad intimidating.

We shook hands, and I apologized for my tardiness. I knew I wasn't making the best impression with my tangled hair, smudged glasses, and dripping makeup, and couldn't help but blush at the state of my disarray.

I began babbling to hide my discomfort. "Conrad is such a great name for a hotel guy. You know, because of Conrad Hilton, the hotelier."

He looked back at me blankly. He either didn't know who I was talking about—but how could he not?—or he'd heard the reference too many times.

"Did you know he was married to Zsa Zsa Gabor, the actress? Only for a few years, though. He was just one of her many husbands." My stepdad, Bob, was a film buff and I'd absorbed a number of Hollywood-related facts from spending time with him. Conrad appeared unimpressed by my knowledge and I quit talking.

He attempted an interested expression. "Uh, huh. I'll show you the kitchen if you're ready. Remind me what you're making."

"Individual cherry meringue tarts, pink velvet cake, and raspberry cream cupcakes."

"Okay. All your ingredients should be ready for you. Remember that we also need you to make heart-shaped sugar cookies for the lobby for tomorrow afternoon and Valentine's Day on Monday. A few dozen both times. The café has already supplied chocolate chip cookies for today."

"Of course." I followed him into the kitchen.

"Check in with the kitchen manager to let her know you're here," Conrad said. "That's her, there. Brenda Clarkson."

We parted, and a pretty woman with brown hair, green eyes, and a light dusting of freckles across her nose came toward me.

I put my hand forward for a shake, but she ignored it.

"You're late," she said with a tight expression.

"I know," I responded. "I'm really sorry." I checked my watch. I'd been expected at 3:30 and it was going on 4:15. Brenda gave me a curt nod to acknowledge the apology.

As an introverted HSP—Highly Sensitive Person—I sensed this environment wouldn't prove conducive to my life goal of maintaining a low stress level at all times. I was used to working alone at my own pace. I could schedule my baking for times when I was at my best and take breaks when necessary. Having a boss watch over me with expectations to produce at a certain speed was a daunting prospect. I told myself the weekend was worth the inconvenience; I was helping out a fellow baker *and* I might snag a few new clients.

Brenda gave me a tour of the kitchen and pointed past the sink to the staff restrooms. She showed me my ingredients and told me where to store my belongings. All of the kitchen equipment was state-of-the-art, and my ingredients, including fresh cherries and raspberries and organic heavy whipping cream, were of the highest quality. I couldn't wait to get started.

"Be back here at five sharp," Brenda said, and I nodded.

I fixed myself up in the luxurious bathroom off the lobby, cringing with each comb stroke down my windblown hair. My shoulder-length wavy blond hair was sensitive to combing, particularly when tangled. I proceeded to wash my face, wipe errant mascara from underneath my brown eyes, clean my glasses, and apply lotion from a pretty glass container to my hands.

Once my appearance was halfway decent, I wandered around until I found the hotel's café. Before pushing open the double doors, I glanced inside the ballroom across the way and admired the impressive chandeliers. I promised myself a better look later.

Inside the café, a beautiful mural of the hotel's exterior graced one of the walls and I stood for a moment appreciating it. But I was soon distracted from the décor to a familiar figure waving to me from one of the tables. I blinked my eyes a couple of times to be sure they weren't deceiving me. They weren't. Of all the cafés in all the historic hotels in all the world . . .

"DAD?"

"Hello, Kayla. Fancy meeting you here."

My father wore khakis and a blue button-down shirt. His glasses were falling down his nose, giving him an absent-minded professor look. He was clean-shaven as always, but his brown hair was parted differently from when I last saw him. A glass of soda and a plate with a half-eaten turkey sandwich and a handful of sweet potato fries sat on the table in front of him.

"What in the world are you doing here?" I asked.

"I'm here for the Gourmet and Stay weekend." He wiped his mouth with a paper napkin imprinted with a picture of the hotel, stood, and gave me a hug.

"But you live in Florida," I protested. "If you've come because of me, how did you know I'd be here?"

He sat down. "Your mother told me. I had some time off from work and thought it would be fun if I came to surprise you. Are you surprised? I didn't expect to find you this soon, so you made it really easy on me." He gestured for me to sit across from him.

"Oh, yes. I'm surprised," I said as I settled into the chair on the opposite side of the table. "But it's a working weekend. You've come such a long way and I won't be available."

"I know. Your mother said you'd be working. But I have a friend I've been meaning to visit in Napa, so I'm spending the weekend here and then driving up there in my rental car Tuesday morning. In the meantime, I thought we might squeeze in some time together. And here we are."

Now that we'd established why we were both there, an awkward silence ensued. My dad and I weren't very close. When I was a child, the highly sensitive trait was yet to be widely acknowledged, and he and my mother didn't know how to handle the tantrums I was prone to when overstimulated. Dad sometimes spanked me when I wouldn't calm down. After he moved to Florida following the divorce, I saw him infrequently. We both seemed to prefer it that way.

"How are things?" Dad asked, breaking the silence.

"Fine. You?"

"Fine."

I thought longingly of the book I'd brought for my downtime. I'd planned on reading in the lobby before I was due in the kitchen. Now, instead of relaxing, I was having a conversation with my father, the last person in the world I'd expected to see at a California historic hotel on Valentine's Day weekend.

"What do you want to eat?" Dad asked.

"Eat?"

"That's why you're in the café, right?"

"Right. Yes. I was going to grab something since I'll be working later. I don't know if I'll be able to have dinner."

"I'll go get you something."

He got up before I could tell him what I wanted. While he was gone, I admired the mural again and tried to come to terms with this unexpected meet-up.

Dad returned to the table a few minutes later with the same food and drink he'd purchased for himself and placed everything in front of me. Fortunately, it was exactly what I'd planned to order.

"Thanks." I picked up a sandwich half and took a bite.

"So, you're still doing the baking thing, then?" Dad asked before taking a sip of soda. "Since you're here, I mean."

My bite of turkey sandwich felt dry in my mouth. "Yes. It's what I do. It's my career."

"I imagine your customer service job was more secure."

"It was killing me, Dad. Remember, I sent you the information about being an HSP?"

We HSPs make up fifteen to twenty percent of the population and are always at risk for overstimulation. We process sounds, sights, smells, and tastes deeply. We take rejection and criticism especially hard but tend to be conscientious, empathetic, and creative. Beauty in nature and art often brings us to tears—in a good way.

Though I was a model employee, a customer service job in a room filled with cubicles, noise, fluorescent lights, and lots of pressure was the last job I should have taken. Three years earlier, when my organization's in-house counselor suggested I might have the Highly Sensitive Person trait, I did some research and found a deep connection to psychologist Elaine Aron's work. I decided to leave my job and move to Seaside Shores, a non-gated planned community in Oceanville, where I started my home baking business eight months later. It was a good decision for my well-being. I was a much happier person now, but not everyone understood how I could give up a steady paycheck.

Dad chewed on a fry. "I got the information. I have it in the condo somewhere."

He followed this up with, "Seen Adam?" and my stomach dropped. I wished he hadn't brought up my ex. He had always liked Adam, even though they'd met just twice. Both golfers, they had bonded over the game. They'd also teamed up to "tease" me about my sensitivity.

I said, with as much authority as I could, "No, I haven't seen him, and I'm not going to, Dad. We broke up. I have a new boyfriend now."

At least I *thought* I had a new boyfriend. Now I was having flashbacks to my college philosophy class: If you only spoke to your boyfriend once a week, and saw him even less than that, were you really together?

Jason Banks, owner of the seafood restaurant Fishes Do Come True at the end of Oceanville Wharf, had recently told me he loved me after a mere two months of dating. I'd freaked out and asked for some space. Once we reunited, we couldn't seem to get back in the groove. It was another reason I'd agreed to take over for Amanda. This way, I could escape the loaded expectations of Valentine's Day. For all I knew, Jason had planned to propose. As much as I liked him and cared for him, he was going a bit fast for me.

I told Dad, "Jason's a restaurateur."

He raised his eyebrows, leaving no doubt what he thought about *that*. Dad was a big believer in job security and loyalty to a company. An accountant, he'd already put in forty years at the same firm and showed no signs of retiring.

For the next fifteen minutes as we ate, we discussed the hotel, the state's baseball teams, and a few current events. Whenever we edged into personal matters—my cats, his golf game—the conversation fell flat as we tried and failed to find common ground.

It was time for me to report to the kitchen. I thanked Dad for the early dinner and said good-bye, promising to find him before I drove home for the night.

In the kitchen, I stashed my messenger bag and washed up, said hello to Brenda, and introduced myself to the other chefs, who had beaten me there. Edward Winthrop, slender and handsome with chiseled features, barely glanced my way while telling me his name. Christie Nelson, who had a cute short haircut I immediately envied, came across as irritated. She reluctantly gave up her name. Hugo Xavier, a wiry twenty-something, shook my hand after introducing himself.

Directed by Brenda, we put on white aprons and black chef's jackets and hats. Like the other cooks, I'd come to work in non-skid shoes and cotton pants, as Conrad had advised.

"I'll be back soon," Brenda said and left.

As the four of us got settled, I picked up a palpable tension in the air, which I didn't understand. We were not in some sort of competition. We were working together as the "Gourmet" part of the Gourmet and Stay weekend.

Christie snapped at Edward when they wanted the same workstation, and Hugo told her to calm down, raising her ire further.

Then Edward said, "How did you people get these jobs? You're a bunch of amateurs!" We hadn't even started cooking yet.

I remained quiet. I planned on staying under the radar all weekend. Plus, I didn't want any bad feelings getting in the way of making the best desserts possible. Many cooks, myself included, believed that emotions could be translated into their food, good *and* bad.

Familiarizing ourselves to the kitchen, the other cooks and I gathered our supplies and brought them back to our workstations, running into each other every few seconds. Christie and Hugo bumped their rear ends, eliciting a crude remark from Edward.

I couldn't help speaking up: "Edward, is that really necessary?"

"Butt out. I can take care of myself," Christie barked at me.

I put my hands up in an appeasing gesture. I had my own problems—I couldn't open the package of heart-shaped mini tart pans, which were embalmed in hard plastic packaging.

"Do we have shears?" I asked the room.

"Here," Hugo said, handing over a pair. "I think these are the only ones."

I opened the package and put the shears back on the center island so we could all reach them. Things became blissfully quiet. No arguments and no insults.

Orders for the various courses before my desserts started pouring in. I made initial preparations for my tarts, cake, and cupcakes, while the others put together appetizers, soups, salads, and entrees. Brenda and the waitstaff, as well as Conrad—who had donned a chef's hat to add finishing garnishes and check the plates—were in and out, and we soon established a rhythm. The other chefs and I managed to not get in each other's way as we constantly traveled from workstation to stove to refrigerator. We were in the zone and focused on our dishes.

My first orders came in. I whipped egg whites and scooped the foam onto eight cherry-filled tarts I'd finished earlier. Five minutes later, I retrieved the batch from the oven, pleased to see the meringues on top were nicely browned. I'd practiced my recipes many times over the last few days to the point that I had them memorized, but you never knew what could happen with an unfamiliar oven.

I removed the tarts from their pans, plated each dessert onto a red dish, and added a dollop of whipped cream to the side. Brenda gave me an appreciative glance as the waitstaff took them away.

Conrad came into the kitchen, beamed a smile at us, and said, "Well done, everyone. The guests are thoroughly enjoying their meals. I've never seen the dining room in such high spirits or the hotel so well-showcased. This weekend is going to be great for business."

An hour later, I was feeling pretty good and Conrad once more was raving to us about how well everything was going. Then the wind howled, the windows shook, and all the lights went out. I almost dropped the cupcakes I'd just removed from the oven. I managed to slip the pan onto the counter.

"No one panic," Conrad said into the darkness. "The generator will kick on soon. It's a good one. It powers most of the hotel."

Sure enough, a few seconds later, the lights came back on.

Unfortunately, one light perfectly illuminated Edward facedown on the floor near the center island, the kitchen shears lodged in the back of his neck.

CHAPTER 2

Several of us screamed. One scream may have been mine. Nothing was getting through to my brain. I was dimly aware of Hugo rushing to Edward to try to remove the shears, but the scene seemed far away from me.

"Don't do that, you idiot!" Christie yelled.

Hugo froze in place and looked over at Christie. "But what if he's not dead?"

"Then you could kill him by taking them out," Christie volleyed back. She pulled Hugo away by grabbing at his shirt.

"Who did this?" This was Brenda. Conrad stood next to her with his mouth open, seemingly unable to speak or move. I knew how he felt.

When no one said anything, Brenda took charge. "Chefs, stay exactly where you are. Do not move. Conrad, check on Edward. Do your best to stabilize the shears until I get help. I'll call 911 and see if I can find a doctor. I'll have the front desk staff clear the guests from the dining area and escort them to their rooms." Her directive spurred Conrad to action. He grabbed a few dish towels and hurried to Edward while Brenda scurried away, her phone already to her ear.

I averted my eyes from Edward and Conrad and took several deep breaths, hoping for the best. My teeth chattered and I wished I were wearing more clothes.

Brenda returned quickly with three hotel security officers and a woman in a cocktail dress holding a medical bag. Conrad moved aside and the doctor bent to Edward to examine him. She looked up at Conrad and shook her head, mouthing "It's too late."

MY HEART HAMMERED AGAINST MY CHEST. I unfortunately had some experience with dead bodies, but I'd never been in the room before when the murder actually took place. It was quite horrible.

"Take the chefs into the conference room," Brenda said, gesturing to the security officers. To Christie, Hugo, and me, she added, "Please remove the clothing we provided and leave everything with me. Retrieve all your personal items."

We did as she asked, then left the kitchen with the security officers. Single file, we crossed the lobby to the conference room, where Hugo, Christie, and I took chairs at the long table in the middle of the room. The security officers remained standing.

The other chefs and I stared at each other—whether for guidance or in accusation, I wasn't sure. The wind howled again and the three of us swiveled our heads to the window. It had been dark for a while now, but the outside lights running off the generator lit up the oak trees in a ghostly manner.

Conrad and Brenda came into the room a few minutes later. Brenda held a tray with the makings for tea and coffee. She placed the tray down on the table a little too hard. The china cups rattled on their saucers.

I knew *I* had not murdered Edward, but goose bumps broke out on my arms as I wondered who had. None of us knew each other. Then I reconsidered. Did I actually know that, or had I only assumed? Edward had made a comment about us being amateurs. He and I had never met, but perhaps he'd known Christie and Hugo.

"The cor—" Conrad stopped to clear his throat. "The coroner and police will be here soon. Edward's body will be removed, and the police will want to talk to each of you."

"We expect your full cooperation," Brenda added.

The two exited the room.

I tried to calm myself down by concentrating on my breathing. Christie and Hugo helped themselves to the materials on the tray and each made a cup of coffee. I felt too queasy to drink anything. The wind picked up even further, and a slamming of something against the outside of the hotel made us all look again out the window. All I could think about now was how much I wished I hadn't taken on this job.

After a wait of what seemed like hours, Conrad came back into the room.

"All right. Here's what's going on," he said. "Trees and branches are down all over the city from the windstorm. The road to the hotel is blocked. No one's getting in or out tonight. As soon as everything's cleared tomorrow, law enforcement will arrive, and we'll go forward with the interviews. You can go to your rooms now. A security officer will be stationed outside your doors."

His last statement in particular got my attention. Because of Flour's problem eye, I hadn't accepted the free room I'd been offered for the weekend. Where would I sleep?

"Conrad?" I said. "I'm commuting. I don't have a room. May I have one?"

"I'm afraid there aren't any available. We're completely booked. I've had to put up staff in the rooms we keep in reserve since they can't go home. The only empty room is, well, Edward's. But I think we better not touch it." He added after a beat, "You're welcome to sleep in the lobby. The couches are quite comfortable."

I didn't know about that. I thought about asking Conrad for a blanket and pillow but decided against it. He had more important things going on.

Security officers led Christie and Hugo out the door. I stumbled into the lobby, trailing my own security officer, who introduced herself as Nina. I was happy to find my father walking around, apparently looking for me.

"Thank goodness," I said. "A friendly face."

"What in the world happened?" he asked. "I'm not supposed to be roaming around, but I was worried about you. Are you all right?

You're shivering." He took off his suit jacket and wrapped it around my shoulders.

"I'm okay, I think."

"So what's going on? The guests have been floating wild theories like a psychotic killer loose in the hotel or some kind of terrorist threat."

"Closer to the first. One of the chefs was stabbed to death when the lights were out and no one knows who did it. I was in the kitchen when it happened. I'll have to be questioned by the police when they're able to get here."

A look of surprise passed over his face. He turned to address Nina. "Who should I talk to about this?"

Before she could answer, I said, "Dad, I just want to go to bed. But I don't have a room. I'm gonna have to sleep here in the lobby."

"That's no good. You can stay with me. I have two double beds."

I asked Nina, "Is that okay?"

"I don't see why not," she said.

"I'm on the fifth floor," Dad said. "The generator's powering one of the elevators." He led us to the nearest bank of elevators and we went upstairs.

Outside the room, Dad and I wished Nina a good evening. I felt a stab of guilt knowing she would probably have to stand all night.

The room was nice, with comfortable-looking furnishings and a gorgeous mural of the hotel grounds spanning the wall behind the two double beds. I would have been delighted to be staying here if it weren't for the circumstances . . . and my roommate. Dad and I hadn't been alone in a room together in years. Whenever he visited me, we went out to eat and met at the restaurant. This was a new experience for us both.

Sensing my unease, he said, "We always shared a room on our trips to Disneyland, remember?"

I remembered, but the memories were not always good. The smell of Dad's cologne, ever present. Scratchy sheets and hard pillows, no matter which motel we stayed in. The noise of an overhead fan and my father's snoring. Dad and Mom sniping at each other.

But I had more immediate problems. "Dad, I just realized. I don't have any overnight things. No nightgown, no toothbrush. Nothing." I took off his jacket and handed it back to him.

"The hotel provided a complimentary toiletries kit. There's a toothbrush and toothpaste, and you can wear one of my shirts to bed. Does that work?"

I nodded. I had a comb and a few cosmetic items in my messenger bag that I always kept with me, so I could make do. Dad laid aside his jacket and rummaged around in his luggage. He passed me a long-sleeved tee shirt that looked like it could cover two of me, and I retrieved my things from my messenger bag.

"You can use the bathroom first. The kit's in there already," he said.

In the bathroom, I used the provided toothbrush and paste to clean my teeth. I found makeup remover tissues in the kit and wiped off my mascara, then used the nice-smelling soap from the dish to wash my face.

After five more minutes, I was ready for bed. I exited the bathroom wearing Dad's shirt, which came down to my knees, and he went in.

I climbed into the bed closest to the window, removed my glasses, and stared at the ceiling, trying to absorb what had happened that evening. Flashes ran through my head without forming a coherent whole—the browned meringues on my tarts, the lights going out, a body, screams . . .

Dad came out of the bathroom wearing plaid pajamas.

"Your tart was delicious, by the way," he said.

"You had one?"

"Yes. I'd about finished up when we received word to leave the dining room. The whole meal was first-rate, but the dessert was the best of all."

I couldn't remember the last time he had given me a compliment. "Thanks, Dad."

Dad approached my bed and touched my foot under the covers. "How are you holding up?"

"Not great. The victim was young, probably my age. I feel awful that he's dead. And I don't like being part of a murder investigation."

"I'm not thrilled by this whole business, myself." Dad sat on the edge of the double bed next to mine. "Do you remember when we used to read Agatha Christies?"

"I do, yeah." During my preteen and early teenage years, Dad and I engaged in what I deemed "The Christie Project." Every month, we chose a book from Christie's extensive body of work, checked out two copies from the library, and read for hours next to each other on the couch. We'd have spirited discussions afterward, and if a film came on TV based on one of the novels we'd read, we would tune in. I hadn't thought of The Christie Project in years and was happy to know that my childhood held *some* good memories of my dad.

"Let's figure this thing out, the two of us," Dad said, his face lighting up. He went to the head of the bed and arranged the pillows so he could sit against them.

"I don't know, Dad. I was involved in a murder case a couple of months ago. It was stressful, to put it mildly."

"Your mother told me about that. Why didn't you let me know? That must have been a major life event for you."

"I'm sorry. I should have."

"It sounds like you were in a lot of danger."

"Yes. But I'm fine now."

Dad took off his glasses, placed them on the nightstand next to his bed, and said, "Let's give it a try, shall we?"

"Okay."

"No one saw who did it?" he asked.

"No. It happened when the lights were out. The killer seized an opportunity, I guess. What's weird is that nothing led up to it. No one had been arguing with the victim. When we first got to the kitchen, there was a little squabbling but nothing terrible."

"Who was there at the time of the murder? What were their roles?"

"Well, there was me and three other chefs. Christie did the appetizers, Hugo made salads and soups, and Edward, the victim, was in charge of the main courses. Both Brenda, the kitchen manager, and Conrad, the hotel owner, were there when the lights went off and when they came back on a few seconds later."

"What about waitstaff?"

I shook my head. "They were in the dining room that whole time."

"Bussers? Dishwashers?"

"The waitstaff bussed their own tables. There was a dishwasher—his name is Frank—but Brenda had asked him to go to the laundry room to get more napkins right before the lights went out."

"So the killer has to be one of those four people you mentioned."

"It looks that way, although it's unlikely Conrad did it. He'd been gushing over how well everything was going and how great it would be for the hotel's bottom line. Why would he put all that in jeopardy?"

"Good point. What about the weapon?"

"A pair of kitchen shears. Each of the chefs used them. Brenda touched them too, I bet. They're no doubt covered in fingerprints."

"What about other DNA?"

"I'm sure everyone's DNA is all over the kitchen, probably even on Edward's body. We brushed against each other several times during dinner prep." I paused. "Brenda took back our aprons and chef's hats and jackets, but I don't think Edward's blood is on any of it. From what I could tell, there wasn't much bleeding. The shears were in his neck and stemming the flow." I shuddered as I recalled the gory sight.

"Doesn't sound like the crime scene investigators will get very far. Who was nearest the victim when the lights came back on?"

I had to think about that. "No one in particular. It was all so quick. I think the killer must have been close to both the shears and Edward when the lights went out. And then moved away fast."

My stomach did a fair imitation of a California black bear's growl.

Dad chuckled. "Hungry?"

"Yeah. The sandwich earlier must not have filled me up. I can't believe I have an appetite after what happened."

"They were going to put out sandwiches and snacks in the café for people who didn't get to finish their meals. I'll run down and get you something."

He hooked his glasses over his ears. Grabbing a sweatshirt from his open suitcase and sliding his feet into a pair of slippers, he left the room.

While he was gone, I realized I could use the time to call my best friend, Isabella Valera, to ask if she'd take care of my cats in the morning. I put on my glasses, retrieved my cell phone from my messenger bag, and made the call.

"Kayla, are you okay? Is something wrong?" Isabella sounded sleepy. I checked the time. Ten-thirty. Whoops.

Talking over the facts of the murder with Dad was one thing. Working through my feelings about what happened while I was already overstimulated was another. The conversation with Isabella was best had in person when I was better rested and I'd had time to process my emotions. I would share with her when I got back to Oceanville.

"Hey, Iz, I'm okay," I said. "Sorry to wake you. The wind's knocked down trees here at the hotel and the roads are blocked. I have to stay overnight. Could you please give the cats breakfast tomorrow morning? And check on Flour's eye?"

"No problem," she said and yawned. "I'll go before work."

"You're the best. Go back to sleep. Thank you." We said goodnight and hung up.

I'd told Jason I would keep in touch over the weekend, but I wasn't ready to tell him about the murder, either. I sent him a text saying I had something to talk about and would come to the restaurant as soon as I could. We might not be in the best place in our relationship, but I could use his support once I'd calmed myself down.

When I was already feeling overwhelmed, even little things bothered me. The seams of Dad's shirt felt scratchy against my skin. Several of my nails were ragged and I didn't know where my file was. I reminded myself that I was alive, while Edward was not.

Dad came back a few minutes later with a banana for himself and a turkey sandwich for me.

Something snapped when he handed me the snack. "Why do you *always* assume I want turkey sandwiches?"

Looking alarmed, he took the sandwich back. "Do you not want turkey? I made your school lunches every day for years. It was the only kind of sandwich you liked. However, I realize you aren't a child anymore, so you're right. I should have asked."

A warm and fuzzy feeling crossed my heart. "You made my lunches? I didn't know that." I was embarrassed now by my outburst.

"Yep. Division of labor. Your mom cleaned up from dinner and I packed your lunch for the next day. Turkey on sourdough with mayonnaise. Never mustard. Never tomatoes. You went through periods when you were okay with lettuce and other periods when you were not. You always liked a bag of chips to go along with your sandwich and a cookie if we had any."

"Well, thank you."

"*Well*, you're welcome. Now do you want this sandwich or not?"

I grinned. Dad took the chair from the desk in the room's sitting area and pulled it over to the coffee table. I did the same with the other chair, which had been facing the TV, and we sat down.

"I'm sorry you have to share your room," I said in between bites.

"I'm not," Dad said with a smile. "I'm glad we get to spend time together. I've missed you. You never want to come to Florida." His smile faded.

"I know. I'm not a big fan of traveling long distances."

"Because you're an HPS?"

I laughed. "HSP. Right. Very good."

"Thanks. Now, I have something important to tell you."

"What's that?"

"I overheard a couple talking while I was in the café. I think it must have been Christie and Hugo because two security officers were hanging around them. To cover, I made a big show of looking over the sandwiches and muttering to myself like some demented old man. The plaid pajama bottoms and slippers added to the effect."

I leaned forward. "You're hardly old. What did they say?"

"I got the feeling that Christie and Edward had been in a relationship at one time. Hugo said perhaps he was more her type than her ex had been, and Christie essentially told him to go to hell."

"No kidding?"

"Yep. Our first clue."

A bubble of anxiety rose up in my chest. We weren't talking about fiction anymore. This was real and potentially dangerous. I wasn't at all sure we should get involved. Fortunately, Dad was distracted by another wind gust, and the subject turned to the weather.

CHAPTER 3

A FTER DAD AND I FINISHED EATING and talking, we agreed it was time to go to sleep. I took my chair out to Nina and she thanked me profusely. Back in the room, I turned off the lights and got into my bed. Dad had already settled into his and pulled the covers up to his chin.

After a few minutes, he said, "Are you still awake, K-Bear?"

I smiled at the nickname, touched that he remembered. My mom had called me "K-Bear" throughout my childhood because of a stuffed polar bear I loved. Every night, I'd hold the soft toy to my face while I tried to fall asleep.

"Yes, I'm awake," I said. "A lot happened today. It'll take me a while to fall asleep."

"I feel the same way. Do you want to talk for a bit?"

"Sure."

"What should we talk about?" he asked.

"I didn't know you and Mom were in touch. She's never mentioned it. How often do you call each other?"

"Probably a couple of times a month. We bear each other no ill will. And we share a daughter that we're both very fond of, you know."

Again, the warm and fuzzy feeling enveloped me. Had I misjudged my dad all these years?

"Tell me about your beau," he said. "His name is Jason?"

"Yeah, Jason Banks. He's great. He's supportive of everything I do. And he's terrific about understanding when my HSP tank is full."

"Why isn't he here with you?"

I hesitated, not sure how to explain what was going on with Jason and me.

"Did something happen between the two of you?" Dad asked.

"He told me he loves me."

"And this was a problem?"

"Well, it was nice to hear, but we'd only known each other for two months."

"I see," Dad said. "But did you know that men in general profess their love sooner than women do?"

"No. Really?"

"Yes. Contrary to popular belief, men fall in love faster and say 'I love you' earlier in a relationship."

I considered this. "It was pretty soon, Dad."

"Maybe, maybe not. A lot depends on whether *you* love *him*. Do you?"

The question I'd been asking myself since January. All I could come up with was an inadequate "I don't know."

"Okay," he said. "I might be able to help. Do you want to take a little quiz? It's something a colleague taught me." When I didn't answer right away, he said, "Indulge me."

"All right." I sat up and put the pillows behind my back. Dad did the same, but we kept the lights off.

"What are three things you love about Jason? There are things you love, yes?"

"Of course."

"They should be qualities that don't have anything to do with you. You've already implied that he treats you well."

"He does."

"So . . . three items exclusive of his relationship with you."

I looked up at the dark ceiling to form my thoughts. "He's exceptionally kind. To everyone he meets."

"Good. What else?"

"He has a great sense of humor."

"Always important. And third?"

"There's so much. I like that he's open-minded. He's willing to change his opinion. To learn different ways of thinking about an issue."

"Excellent."

"Is that it? Does that mean I love him?"

"We're not done yet," Dad said. "Now I want you to give me three things you *don't* like about him."

"This is part of it?"

"Yes. Be honest."

"He can be messy. Extremely messy. His apartment is a disaster."

"You should see my condo. Go on."

"He's something of a workaholic. He gets obsessed. But he does own a restaurant. There's a lot to do. It's open seven days a week."

"That's understandable, then. And third?"

I pondered for a few seconds. "I don't know. I can't think of anything at the moment."

"Are the two things you named deal-breakers? Are they things you would want to change about him?"

"No. As flaws go, they aren't bad. What does it mean, Dad?"

"It's up to you, sweetheart. Only you can decide."

I turned this over in my head. I loved so much about Jason. As Dad's "quiz" had proven, I was hard-pressed to come up with things I *didn't* love. I thought about him all the time, was happy for his successes, and wanted to share every part of my life with him. It was clear—I loved him and should tell him that. So why hadn't I done it yet?

"Kayla, I have a feeling your mother's and my divorce is making you gun shy."

"That's possible, but what happened with Adam also affected me. He may have tolerated my sensitivity at the beginning of our relationship, but he never truly accepted it. That hurt me."

"I'm guilty of that as well, I suppose," Dad said. "I knew things bothered you when you were small. I shouldn't have handled it the way I did."

This was the closest he'd ever come to an apology for the spankings he'd given me. He was different from what I remembered. More empathetic. Kinder. Perhaps the darkness was loosening his tongue. Or . . .

"Dad, have you been dating?"

"Off and on. Now there's someone special. I feel she's softening me."

"Who is she?" I asked. "What's she like?"

"Her name is Stacy. She was a high school biology teacher. Retired now. She loves to play tennis and golf. She enjoys baking. I think the two of you would hit it off."

"It would be nice to meet her sometime."

"Then we'll have to arrange that."

"Okay. I'm going to try to sleep now. Good-night, Dad."

"Good-night, honey."

I fluffed the pillows and turned onto my right side. I was wide awake and all too aware of what had occurred earlier in the evening. I tried rolling onto my left side, then lying on my back. Nothing helped. Although the hotel room was lovely and Dad and I were getting along, what I dearly wanted was my own bed in my own house, and the time and space to reflect on what had happened. I didn't fall asleep until way after midnight.

DAD AND I WOKE AT THE SAME TIME and bid each other good morning. I put on my glasses and checked the wall clock. It was a few minutes after seven.

I got up out of bed and walked over to the window. Our room was on the same side of the hotel as the entrance. Branches littered the front lawn, attesting to the power of the wind the night before. Now there wasn't even a breeze. I wondered if the power was back on or if the hotel was using the generator.

I noticed a piece of paper on the carpet near the door. I went over and picked it up.

"What's that?" Dad asked as he climbed out of bed and stretched.

"It's from the hotel. The power's back on. Breakfast will be available beginning at nine in the café. I wonder when they'll clear the roads and the police will come." The thought got my stomach churning.

"Are you hungry now?" Dad asked. "I have a big bag of nuts from the airport in my bag."

"Sure, I'd love some."

He dug into his luggage and passed a bag of nuts to me. I held the bag open and we each took a handful of almonds.

"We could watch TV until breakfast," Dad said. "Your choice. An Agatha film might be on."

As I chewed on a few nuts, I located the remote and turned on the TV. I surfed the channels and found a repeat episode of *Premier Chef*, a show that had debuted the fall before.

"A reality show?" Dad said.

"You said I could choose."

"That's right, I did."

"I've never seen it. I don't get this channel. I watch all the other cooking shows, though. It's so inspiring to see chefs learn and grow and follow their dreams."

He looked at me thoughtfully. "Is that what you're doing?"

"I've got to have creativity in my life. My customer service job wasn't fulfilling that need for me. I know it's risky to own my own business, but baking is my . . ."

I stopped talking as something on the show caught my attention.

"Dad. See that guy there? It's Edward, the victim. And there's Brenda, the kitchen manager. They knew each other before this weekend."

Dad got closer to the TV and peered at the screen. "That's an interesting development."

"I'm gonna sign up for a streaming service on my phone and watch all the episodes," I said. "I want to start at the beginning and see this whole season. Maybe I'll figure something out." So much for not getting involved in Edward's murder case.

"Fine by me. But I don't think I'll join you. I'm going to clean myself up and read a book. Let me know if you come up with anything."

"Sounds good."

AFTER NINETY MINUTES OF SKIMMING all eight episodes of the show, I knew two things: 1., Edward's arrogance had been on full display throughout the competition as he talked back to the judges even when they praised him, and 2., despite his overconfidence, he finished runner-up to Brenda, who was crowned Premier Chef.

I told Dad.

He put aside his book and straightened his glasses. "That's good. So, not only were they in the competition together, they were the number one and number two finishers. That could be significant."

"Yeah, but the two didn't have much interaction until the final episode. In the team challenges, they were never paired together. When they did have contact with each other, it was civil."

"Does the runner-up get any money or prizes?"

"Money, yes," I replied. "I looked it up. But not nearly as much as the winner. Edward and Brenda may have gotten into a fight about that before dinner prep, and Brenda took the opportunity of the power outage to stab him. I'd say we have possible motives for both Christie and Brenda, Monsieur Poirot."

"And I would agree, Miss Marple."

AFTER I SHOWERED, I DRESSED in my cotton pants and blouse from the day before and smeared on some lipstick from a tube I unearthed from my messenger bag. As I was putting on my shoes, I received a text from Conrad summoning me to the conference room.

"I think this is it," I said to Dad.

"You'll do fine." He came over to me and touched my forearm. "All you have to do is tell the truth. You have nothing to hide."

"Right. Thanks."

"It's just turned nine. I'll get breakfast for us while you're talking to the police."

We went out the door and greeted Nina. She looked exactly as she had the night before, her uniform immaculate and her dark hair tied back in a sleek ponytail. I was impressed.

Dad and I smiled at her.

"How was your night?" I asked.

"Tolerable because of the chair. Thank you again."

Dad took the chair back into the room and returned. Nina followed us as we headed downstairs. Dad went in the direction of the café and Nina and I entered the conference room.

Christie, Hugo, Conrad, and Brenda were already there, as were the other security escorts. Only Christie and Hugo were seated. I took the chair next to Hugo and looked in front of me at a sad collection of packaged muffins, browning sliced bananas and apples, a glass carafe of muddy coffee, and a pitcher of water. Too bad we weren't allowed in the kitchen; the three of us could probably whip up a tasty breakfast. For the first time, it occurred to me that I'd never made the heart-shaped sugar cookies for the lobby. A shiver ran through me as I remembered what had transpired the evening before.

I didn't feel especially hungry after having the nuts, so I decided to hold off on eating until I was with Dad. I poured myself a glass of water and took a long gulp. Christie grabbed a muffin and Hugo helped himself to coffee.

"Okay, we're all here," Conrad said. "Before I begin, I want you to know I'll be writing checks for last night's work. I'll leave them at the front desk for when you're able to leave."

That was nice to hear.

"The roads have been cleared," he went on. "The coroner and police should arrive any minute."

Mere moments later, a knock at the door was followed by the arrival of a number of men and women, some dressed in plainclothes and others in uniform. A tall man with a neatly trimmed mustache and goatee identified himself as Detective David Hernandez, the lead on Edward's murder case. I put my hand to my stomach as it flip-flopped.

"Kayla used the shears," Hugo said right off. "I handed them to her."

I shook my head at him.

"That's exactly right," Christie piped up.

I said, "Christie, I saw *you* using the shears for your artichokes.

After I put them back, by the way. And, Hugo, *you* used them for your basil, didn't you? I didn't even know him. Why would I stab him?"

Det. Hernandez held up his hands. "Okay, okay. You'll have plenty of time to give us your statements. We'll be talking to each of you individually in the meeting rooms." He took a notepad from his pocket, reviewed it, and said, "Sykes, I'd like you to take Mr. Xavier to Meeting Room 1. Paulson, you've got Ms. Nelson in 2. I'll be with Ms. Jeffries in 3." He looked at me. "You're Kayla Jeffries? Come with me, please."

I walked after him to Room 3. We sat kitty corner from each other at the end of a long table. As the detective took off his jacket, I looked around the room. The wall closest to us was almost entirely covered with photos of the hotel's storied history. A large screen on another wall made me wish I were here for some kind of presentation that had nothing to do with murder.

"Can I get you something?" Det. Hernandez asked. "Water? Juice?"

I shook my head. "No, thanks. I had water in the conference room."

He looked down at his notepad. He already had a few basic details about me, including my phone numbers and address, which I guessed he'd gotten from Conrad. I confirmed that everything was correct. He then asked me to tell him, in my own words, what had happened in the kitchen.

Dad had advised me to tell the truth. But should I refuse to talk until I had a lawyer present? I decided to provide information, hoping this could all be wrapped up soon. I spoke, going into as much detail as I remembered: the power outage, the generator, the lights coming back on, Edward's body on the floor . . .

When I was done relaying what had gone on to the best of my knowledge, Det. Hernandez said, "You own a home baking business in Oceanville? Kayla's Home-Baked Goods by the Sea?"

"Yes, that's right."

"It's my understanding you weren't the original dessert chef for the weekend. Can you talk about that?"

"Amanda, the original guest baker, called a few nights ago and asked me to take over for her. I promise you, I now wish I hadn't said yes."

"That would be Amanda Longfellow?"

I agreed.

"How well do you know her?"

"I only met her once, at a convention for bakers in Los Angeles. We hit it off enough to exchange contact details, but we hadn't been in touch until this week. I assume she reached out to other dessert chefs but I don't know. She might have chosen me because I live in the same county as the hotel."

"Why did she want someone to take over?"

I said, "She didn't say, and I didn't ask. It didn't seem important." I wondered if he thought this was significant.

He checked the notes he'd just taken. "You said that when the lights went out, you were taking cupcakes out of the oven?"

"Right. I managed to place the pan onto the counter, mostly by feel. It was dark."

"Do you know where the others were when the lights went out?"

"No. I was aware of who was in the kitchen, as I mentioned before, but everyone was moving around a lot. It was hectic."

"You're certain you didn't see anything? Hear anything?"

"No. Nothing. I'm sorry I can't be more helpful."

Det. Hernandez flashed a smile and said, "You're doing fine. Just a few more questions. You said you didn't know Edward Winthrop. You'd never met him?"

"No." My throat felt dry and I wished I had accepted the offer of something to drink.

"Mr. Xavier and Ms. Nelson said you used the shears. Did you?"

"Yes. All the chefs did. Brenda, the kitchen manager, was also there when the murder happened. She and Edward knew each other, I've found out. I believe Christie might have known him too."

He regarded me. I regarded him back.

He paused for a moment and then said, "You can return to the conference room. Please wait there."

BACK IN THE CONFERENCE ROOM, Christie's and Hugo's expressions were tense. I didn't feel so calm myself. Conrad, Brenda, and the security officers stood by.

Det. Hernandez came into the room a few minutes later.

"How long do we have to stay here?" Christie asked. "If the event is cancelled, I'd like to go home."

"Yeah, dude, me too. This is a load of bullpucky," Hugo said.

"I'm sorry that I've caused you inconvenience," Det. Hernandez told them. "But can you imagine the inconvenience for Edward Winthrop? Since, as you know, he's dead."

Christie and Hugo didn't say a word.

Det. Hernandez motioned to Conrad, who said, "We're giving out refunds and cancelling the weekend. The hotel will be closed until Tuesday. The guests and all but a skeleton staff will be sent home. The three of you will be staying a while longer. You can return to your rooms now. Security, please take them now."

"Wait, Conrad," I said. "Can my dad stay with me? I'm using his room."

Conrad gestured to Det. Hernandez to answer the question. He said, "That's fine."

As Hugo got up from the table, he tripped over his shoelaces before regaining his balance. He grinned at us sheepishly.

Nina accompanied me to the fifth floor, and I went inside the room. Dad was back with hash browns, eggs, and bacon. As we ate, I told him about my interview.

"It wasn't that bad," I said. "He wanted to know if I'd seen or heard anything. I said I hadn't. And I told him I didn't know Edward. I think he believed me."

"That's good," Dad said. "They might not even consider you a possible suspect."

"I hope so. On the other hand, no one said I could go home yet."

"Let's do some research on the others, shall we? We have to get you out of here."

"All right."

I'd turned the volume down on my phone when I went

downstairs for the interview. I turned it up again and checked messages. Isabella had texted to say she'd fed Flour and Sugar and given them fresh water. I texted back to thank her.

A half hour later, Dad and I were knee-deep in following up on our ideas for suspects. So far we'd come up empty, other than confirming that Edward and Brenda had made it to the finals of *Premier Chef*. There was little information on the internet about Brenda at all and she had no social media pages.

I wondered out loud how she ended up a kitchen manager. As *Premier Chef*'s first champion, she appeared to have a bright future in cooking. From what I could tell, she'd gone straight from doing the show to working at the hotel.

"Perhaps she didn't want the pressure of being a chef," Dad suggested.

"Hmm. Could be," I said. "It *is* a stressful job." I was glad I was a baker who worked from home rather than a restaurant chef.

As far as the relationship between Edward and Christie, I'd found nothing. Christie's personal Facebook page was set at the highest privacy settings, and her professional pages held no intimate information.

Although I was able to access the posts on Edward's personal Facebook page, I discovered nothing of interest, other than a message from his mother, Melody, saying how loved her son was and how much he would be missed. The message concluded with an open invitation to a memorial service that coming Thursday at her home in La Tierra, a town coincidentally close to The Countryside Inn.

To a one, the comments under Melody's post were positive. No one said anything at all negative about Edward, but that was to be expected since he'd just died, and his mother could have read it. The comments included condolences from friends, fans, and a number of fellow cooks, including contestants from *Premier Chef*.

Like Brenda, Hugo didn't have much of an internet presence at all, other than a few cooking demos he'd posted on LiveandLearn that I didn't bother viewing. I didn't blame them for shying away from social media. When it came to the internet, I drew the line at a business website, although I knew I could drum up more clients if I dived into Facebook, Twitter, or Instagram.

My phone rang. I checked the caller ID.

"It's Jason," I told Dad. I accepted the call and said, "Hi, there."

"Hi, honey. I got your text. Is everything okay?"

"Yeah, thanks. I'll come to the restaurant to see you when I get a chance."

"Looking forward to it."

"Me too. Have a good rest of the day."

After I hung up, Dad said, "I'm gonna stretch my legs and be back in a bit."

"Okay. Have a good walk."

HE CAME BACK TEN MINUTES LATER, his glasses so far off his nose they were practically in his mouth.

"Guess what?" he said.

"I have no idea. What?"

"You're about to get clearance to leave."

"You're kidding. They found out the killer?"

"I don't think so, but the police can't hold you indefinitely. They must not have the evidence to make an arrest."

I blinked a few times. "Wow. It feels weird, but I assume they'll still be investigating."

"I'm sure they will. We can go back to our real lives for now. I'm going to head on to Napa. I already called my hotel and they can accommodate me early. You can go on home and hopefully put this behind you."

Dad and I were soon ready to go and went down to the lobby. Before leaving, I picked up my check from the front desk clerk. I didn't see Conrad, so I asked her to tell him I'd left and to thank him for hiring me. I hoped he was doing okay. I'd send him an email when I got home.

In the hotel lot, Dad turned to me. "I guess this is good-bye for now, K-Bear." Unbeknownst to me, I'd parked next to his car. I wondered if it was a sign.

"Take care, Dad," I said, giving him a hug. Tears sprang to my eyes and I wiped them away.

"Don't cry, honey," he said. "I'll call you soon."

We got into our cars. Dad drove off first, waving to me as he exited the lot. I took a moment before leaving, marveling at the fact that I missed him already. Who would have guessed?

CHAPTER 4

THERE WAS LITTLE TRAFFIC GOING HOME, and I was able to relax and come back to myself in the solitude. I turned the radio to a music station and kept it at a low volume. Right before I arrived into Oceanville, however, a story about the murder came on the news at the top of the hour.

"Hugo Xavier, Christie Nelson, and Kayla Jeffries, the other chefs hired for the weekend, were in the kitchen at the time of the murder, along with the kitchen manager, Brenda Clarkson, and the owner of the hotel, billionaire Conrad Cunningham. All have been interviewed by Los Robles police. Xavier works at a restaurant in Greenbrook, Nelson is the former owner of the defunct Abalone in San Diego, and Jeffries runs a baking business out of her home in Oceanville. Turning to traffic . . ."

"What the heck?" I muttered. This was an unwelcome development. Was the news of the murder—and my name—everywhere?

Although anxious to see my cats, particularly Flour because of her eye, I decided to go talk to Isabella first. I was ready to share what had happened the night before and I wanted her input on the radio story. Once I reached Seaside Shores, I turned onto the road for the clubhouse restaurant and swung into the parking lot.

The restaurant, formally known as The Seaside Waves, was a popular meeting place for the community's residents. The menu ranged from specialty coffee drinks to casual sandwiches to high-end entrees—something for everyone. Isabella had worked there since college and was both a well-liked and outspoken waitress.

"How are the cats?" I asked as soon as she broke away from chatting at a table with her neighbors, Donald and Mary Cohen. "What about Flour's eye?"

"They're fine," she said. "Flour's eye looks okay to me. I'm touched that you asked after them before finding out how *I* am."

"I'm sorry, Iz. How are you?"

"Well, I'm sleepy. You woke me up last night."

"I'm really sorry about that too. I'll tell you all about it if you can take a break."

"Sure. Decaf iced coffee? It's warm outside. A heat wave in February, can you believe it?"

"Climate change," we said at the same time.

A few minutes later, we were settled in our seats at a table overlooking the water.

"Why are you here, anyway?" Isabella asked. "Don't you have to do desserts for lunch today? Is it because of the windstorm?" She took out her ponytail band and rearranged her abundance of dark curls.

"You won't believe this, but there was a murder at the hotel. They cancelled the rest of the weekend."

Her eyes grew wide. "A murder? Another one? You've got to be kidding me. Are you okay?"

"I'm okay. Better than I was last night. I was there at the time, and it was scary and awful. The victim was young. My age."

"Who was it?"

"A chef named Edward Winthrop. He was stabbed with a tool we'd all used."

"That's so horrible. Who killed him?"

"No one knows. The power went out from the windstorm and the killer used the darkness as cover." I took a long sip of iced coffee, which Isabella had thoughtfully loaded up with sugar. She'd also provided some of the chocolate cake I'd delivered to the restaurant the day before I left for Los Robles. The restaurant was a new client for me but a steady one.

"That's unreal," Isabella said, shaking her head.

"I know. But here's another thing. I just heard about it on the radio. They gave my name and said I own a home bakery. I didn't know that would come out. What if my regular clients bail on me because they think I might be the murderer? What if no one new wants to hire me?" I turned my opal birthstone ring around on my finger.

"I'm sure people who know you will realize you had nothing to do with it."

"I don't think I can take any chances. I have to figure out who's responsible."

Isabella raised her eyebrows at me. "You're going to voluntarily become involved in another murder investigation?"

"I kind of already did. My dad was at the hotel, and we were trying to work it out. He wanted to relive our days of reading Agatha Christies."

"Whoa, what? Back up. Your bio dad? The one who lives in Florida? Not your stepdad?"

"Yes. He showed up to surprise me."

"I never would have expected that."

"Me, neither," I said. "But it was okay. Better than okay. We got along surprisingly well."

Almost imperceptibly, Isabella's expression darkened. I sensed she was thinking about her own father, who had died in a car crash when she was only thirteen. The accident had killed her mother too. I touched her hand across the table and she gave me a small smile.

She straightened her shoulders as if shaking off the sad thoughts, and said, "What about Jason? What did he say about it?"

"We talked briefly but I haven't told him anything yet. I'll go see him later."

"I don't think he's gonna like you investigating," she said. "Not after what happened last year."

I knew she was right, but I didn't have the emotional energy to ponder that now. I decided to change the subject. "How's Brian?"

Isabella's boyfriend, Brian, was a detective with the Oceanville Police Department. He and I had a complicated relationship. He hadn't liked me getting involved in the murder investigation of my friend, Trudy, the year before, but because I'd cracked the case, he now held a grudging respect for me. At least I hoped that to be true. It's not as though he'd ever said it explicitly.

"He's fabulous," Isabella said, a smile breaking out all over her face. "We're going out tomorrow night for Valentine's. He's surprising me. I don't know where we're going yet." She did a little dance in her seat.

"And studying?"

Twenty-nine-year-old Isabella was scheduled to take the law school admission test in July. She had a degree in women's studies from UC Oceanville and was hoping to become a women's rights attorney once she passed the Bar.

"It's going well, mostly because of your gift," she said. "Thank you again. Best present ever."

I'd given her admission to an online LSAT prep course for Christmas. I told her I was glad it was helping.

After we finished our cake and coffee, I said I'd better get home.

"Stay safe," Isabella said. "Call if you need anything, sweetie." One of the many things I adored about my best friend was the way she called me "sweetie" and "hon," though I was more than five years older.

"Thanks, Iz." We said good-bye and I set out for home. On the way, I drove by houses painted in different shades of blues and greens with touches of white. I loved that all the residences in Seaside Shores were painted in the colors of the sea. My beloved oceanside community always lifted my spirits, and its beauty almost made me forget I'd been a witness to a murder.

I turned into my driveway, drove past my landlord's house, and parked outside my teal cottage. I grabbed my messenger bag and hurried up the porch steps to the front door.

My three-year-old American shorthair cats, Sugar and Flour, ran to greet me as I entered the door. They wound themselves around my legs, preventing me from moving. I bent to pet them, and they arched their backs for scratches. I checked Flour's eye, which looked completely back to normal.

"Good news, Flour," I said. "No v-e-t."

The cats followed me as I puttered around the house getting settled. I cleaned their litter box, put away my messenger bag, and sent Conrad a brief email.

Once the chores were done, we returned to the living room and took up residence on the couch, a cat on either side of me. I looked down at them fondly.

I'd inherited the all-white cats a few months before; Sugar from my late friend, Trudy, and Flour from her human family who was moving and unable to keep her. I was crazy about them. The two had added a dimension to my life I'd never imagined and they were a great stress reliever.

After an extended period of feline companionship, I decided it was time to go see Jason. The cats seemed to think we were going to make up for my absence by spending the rest of the day in this exact position, so I had to take charge and get up. Besides, I wanted to change my clothes. I was wearing the same things I'd put on yesterday. I took a shower, threw on fresh jeans, a tee shirt, and a light cardigan, clipped on my sunglasses, and went out the front door.

"Kayla."

It was my landlord, Tristan, and his new boyfriend, Jeremy, owner of SeaBlue Gallery in downtown Oceanville. Tristan, who'd recently shaved his greying beard and mustache, held a large rectangular package wrapped in brown paper. He grinned at me.

I grinned back. "Hi, you guys. How are you? Tristan, I can't believe it. It's ready?"

"I think it's as good as the original, if I do say so myself," Tristan said.

"Better," Jeremy corrected. Jeremy was a few years younger than Tristan, having turned fifty the week before. The front of his light blond hair was hanging in his eyes and he brushed it aside.

We went inside the cottage. Tristan tore off the brown paper and showed me the painting that would replace the one I'd smashed in December. I gasped as soon as he unveiled it.

The original had featured children making sandcastles on the beach, the sun setting in the background. The new painting showed adults and children dressed in old-style clothing riding a carousel by the ocean. It was breathtaking. Tristan's Impressionistic paintings reminded me of Monet's work, and I had yet to come to terms with the fact that he didn't paint all the time—preferring to dabble in other art forms, that for me at least, suffered in comparison.

"Where is this?" I asked. "Is it a real place?"

"Used to be," Tristan said. "It was an amusement park called Oceanville Playworld. And guess what? Seaside Shores was built on the same site years after it was torn down. We visited the history museum in January, and I used some photos we saw for inspiration. I had no idea that our little community was once an amusement park."

"I didn't know, either," I said.

"Playworld was very popular," Jeremy contributed. "It was the place to be in the nineteen twenties through the nineteen forties."

"That is too cool," I said, excited by the idea that I lived where an amusement park once stood.

"We think this is where the dolphin fountain in Alden Park is now," Tristan said, pointing to the carousel. "Isn't the merry-go-round fantastic? I've always wanted to try my hand at designing one."

"It's beautiful. Thank you so much, Tristan, for doing this. I appreciate it more than I can say. But you've now given me two paintings. Can't I pay you?"

He shook his head. "Never, doll. It just makes me happy that you love it."

We hung the painting over the fireplace. As was his way, Tristan gazed at it in appreciation and I was afraid he might take it back. I thanked him again, promised the two a batch of cherry meringue tarts to express my appreciation, and walked them back to Tristan's house.

"We want to take you to dinner," Jeremy said before they went inside. "Let us know the best night."

"How nice. I'll check my schedule. Thanks."

I decided to hold off on telling them about the murder until we had more time. We said good-bye and I left for Jason's restaurant.

On the walking path that ran parallel to the water for the length of the community and ended at the wharf, I came upon my friend Vicky and her daughter, Angie. A few months earlier, I'd suggested to Vicky that eight-year-old Angie might be an HSP and I'd emailed them some information. It was heartening to see how Angie had blossomed since Vicky had incorporated the knowledge into her parenting. I took note of the softness of Angie's clothes and the heart-shaped sunglasses she wore to block the glare.

"Hi, you two." I bent to give Angie a hug. "How are things?"

Vicky answered, "Good. Getting back into our old routines. We've been in Washington for a few days to visit my brother and his family."

"That sounds fun," I said.

"We stayed at a really neat old hotel," Angie told me.

"No kidding. I was just at an old hotel, myself." Because I didn't want to upset Angie, I didn't say how my hotel stay had gone.

"We've gotta get back," Vicky said. "Clean ourselves up and then get a late lunch."

"We're having veggie pizza," Angie said.

I put my hands on my hips and said, "Oh, my gosh. I am *so* jealous," making Angie giggle.

Vicky patted her daughter's blond curls. "Then we're going to have reading time, right, kiddo?"

"Yeah. I'm reading *Harriet the Spy*," Angie said.

"Oh, I love that book," I replied. "I plan to have reading time soon too." Reading was one of my favorite ways of calming my nervous system.

Vicky put her hand to my arm. "I'll be in touch soon. We're having John's relatives over for his birthday and I could use a dessert. It's on March first."

"You know how to reach me. Give me a call or shoot me an email. See you." They left for home and I headed for the wharf, wondering if I should reread *Harriet the Spy*. Maybe I'd get some ideas for solving Edward's murder.

As I passed by a young couple kissing on a bench overlooking the water, my phone chimed with an email alert. I was surprised to find a cancellation for an Easter dessert party. An Easter dessert party for twenty people which would have netted me a nice paycheck. No reason given. I couldn't help but think the client had heard about my association with Edward's murder. I'd acknowledge the email later that evening.

I was more and more eager to see Jason with each step I took, and after a while wasn't taking in the gorgeous scenery of sea, sand, and shore. But once I reached the door to Fishes Do Come True at the end of the wharf, I was overtaken by what-ifs. What if Jason didn't feel the same way about me anymore? What if he wanted to break up? We hadn't seen each other for almost two weeks and hadn't talked much. I might not be sure how I wanted our relationship to develop nor of my exact feelings for him, but I did know I didn't want to lose him.

Inside the restaurant, I looked around for Jason. I saw him over at a booth, talking and laughing with a family of three. I felt a rush of affection for him. He was so kind. Not to mention smart, funny, and handsome. He had the beginnings of a five o'clock shadow and his dark hair was mussed, somehow making him all the more attractive.

He finished speaking with the patrons, turned, and saw me. I detected a certain wariness in his ocean blues, but he strode over with a big smile on his face. He put his arms around me and pulled me close.

"Hi," he whispered in my ear.

"Hi. It's really good to see you."

"Likewise. Hungry?"

I laughed. "Always."

"Clam chowder in a bread bowl and salad?"

"That sounds great."

"Go out to the deck. It's nice out there. It's not too hot and not too cold, and you've got your sunglasses on."

As I often had felt over the course of our relationship, I was struck by how well he knew me after a relatively short time. He released me and left for the kitchen.

A BRIEF WHILE LATER, Jason and I sipped our drinks and ate our lunches, every so often gazing out at the water. Jason pointed out a couple of otters floating around on their backs.

I slurped down my soup with a singular lack of decorum. I'd forgotten how much I enjoyed Jason's chowder. Since we'd not been seeing each other that often, it had been too long since I'd had any. I was pretty jazzed about the sourdough bread bowl too. Jason was a triple threat—restaurant owner, manager, and creator of the best chowder and bread in Ocean County, at least in my humble opinion. Not to mention an all-around great guy whom I probably loved and should tell as much. I tried to form the words but couldn't seem to do it.

"Not that I'm complaining, but what are you doing here?" Jason asked. "I thought you were booked for the weekend. Aren't you supposed to be finishing up desserts for lunch right about now?"

I let out a long breath. It was time to tell him. "That's what I wanted to talk to you about. Everything was called off. There was an incident at the hotel. A murder."

He threw his head back and laughed. "No, really, why are you back?"

"I'm not kidding. One of the other chefs was stabbed with kitchen shears when the lights were out from the windstorm. No one knows who did it. The other cooks and I had to be interviewed by the police. They couldn't hold us forever without making an arrest, so they let us go."

Jason took a few seconds to absorb this. "That's incredible. I'm so sorry you had to go through that. It must have been very upsetting and stressful for you."

"Yeah. We all saw the body—it was too horrifying for words. And the victim was so young. Then the police couldn't get there until this morning because of the weather. I had to stay overnight. It was excruciating having to wait to be interviewed and then not knowing when I could come home."

"I can imagine. Thank god you weren't hurt and you're safe."

I nodded but remained silent.

"What's the matter, honey? Still trying to process?" He reached across the table and took my hand. "Have you had enough time to work through it?"

"I'm all right. But something happened when I was driving back to Oceanville. I was on the radio in connection with the murder. They identified me and the other chefs who were there. They said I'm the owner of a home baking business."

"I'm sure the police can't seriously be considering you."

"I hope not." I chewed on a piece of bread.

"They'll arrest the killer soon," Jason went on. "There can't be that many people who could have done it, right?"

"Three, if you count the kitchen manager."

"There you go. It's one of those three and the police should be able to narrow that down to one in no time."

"That will be a relief."

"Do you want dessert? I have to place an order soon, by the way. I'm running out of your goodies."

Even during the moratorium on our personal relationship, I'd been delivering desserts to Jason's restaurant. He was one of my best clients.

"No, I'm full, thanks. Let me know what you want, and I'll get started on the order."

"I'll check what's left and get back to you."

"Okay. Jason, the victim's memorial service is on Thursday in La Tierra. I want to go pay my respects and maybe talk to a few people to gather information. Since I'll be in the area, I think I'll stop by the police station and meet with the detective in charge. I've already come up with a couple of motives for the others."

"Kayla, I don't think that's a good—"

"I'm worried about my business. I had a cancellation on the way here. I've got to get my name cleared of having anything to do with the murder."

I could tell from his furrowed brow that he wasn't pleased.

"Say something," I said.

"I understand you're concerned about your business. But it's the police's job to clear you and find the real culprit. Do I have to remind you what happened last time you got involved in an investigation?"

Cue the flashbacks of my house in complete disarray and hands around my neck, squeezing hard. It had taken several weeks for my nervous system to calm down after the events of last year, and I wasn't sure I'd fully recovered.

"I'll be careful if I decide to go," I said.

Jason picked up his glass and took a long sip of soda. My reassurance apparently hadn't convinced him.

"You could go with me?" I suggested.

"I can't. My sous chef isn't in that day. I'd really prefer it if you didn't go. You have to keep out of this. Please."

I half-nodded but didn't answer.

We finished eating but neither of us spoke much. I couldn't believe that once we were on our way to getting back on track, we'd been derailed. He didn't ask to come over to my place that evening and I didn't invite him. I slogged home, half-relieved and half-disappointed that he hadn't brought up Valentine's Day, which was now only hours away.

CHAPTER 5

AT HOME AFTER SEEING JASON, I changed into linen pajama bottoms and checked orders and emails in my office, finding two cancellations from established clients. Had they heard of my connection to Edward's murder? I sent replies to the two, as well as to the woman who'd cancelled the Easter party, then went into the living room and sank into the couch. Sugar jumped onto my lap and started kneading. Her claws went right through my pajama pants, and rather than make her get up, I gritted my teeth and bore it. The things I did for my beloved cats.

To distract myself from the pain, I talked to her about the case. "Okay, Sugar, listen up. I've got to work this out to clear my name and save my business. Hugo is least likely to be the killer, I think. Other than myself, of course. He had no ties to Edward that I could find. Christie and Brenda are both obvious suspects because they knew Edward before the hotel event. I have to make sure Detective Hernandez has considered Brenda. She certainly took charge after the murder. She knew exactly what to do. Would she have had the wherewithal to do that if she'd just killed someone in cold blood? I don't know. If she's a good actress, she might."

Sugar finally stopped kneading and sprawled across my lap. I breathed a sigh of relief. Flour came into the room, looked up at us, and meowed.

"Sorry, I don't think there's room," I told her.

She jumped up next to us and placed a paw on my arm.

"Okay, honey, that's fine. You help too."

Just then my cell phone rang. Reaching around Sugar, I took the phone from my sweater pocket and answered. I was alarmed to learn it was Detective Hernandez.

After we'd greeted each other, he said, "We'd like you to stop by the police station to answer a few more questions. When can you do that?"

More questions? That didn't sound good. But I *had* been planning to go see him anyway. I told him I could come Thursday at ten if that worked for him.

"That will be fine," he said and gave me directions. "See you then."

We hung up and I looked down at the cats.

"I don't know what that's about, but I better have a plan," I said. "First step is to talk to Amanda Longfellow, the baker I took over for, to see if she knows anything. Maybe she knows something she doesn't even know she knows, if you follow me. Second step is seeing Detective Hernandez to answer his questions and give him my ideas. Then I'll go to the service after that and hopefully pick up some helpful information. Third step is . . . I don't know yet. I'll have to think about it."

THE NEXT MORNING, I MADE A CUP OF DECAF COFFEE using my single-serve machine. Finding two scones in the freezer, I warmed them up in the microwave. Breakfast ready, I called Amanda.

As I sipped my coffee and ate a scone, Amanda told me she'd attended her cousin's memorial service on Saturday. She sounded overtaken by grief and had a hard time getting out even this minimal information. After giving her my condolences, I recounted what had happened at The Countryside and she expressed her dismay and shock. She hadn't heard the news yet.

"I'd already decided to take a break from baking and reassess things," she said. "My cousin was young, not that much older than I am. And now Edward is dead. It's a cliché, but we've got to make sure every second counts. I want to be sure I'm doing what's best for my soul." She punctuated the end of her last sentence with a sob.

"That sounds like a good idea to take a break," I said. "I hope it helps. Before you go, is there anything you can tell me about Edward, Hugo, or Christie?"

"Brenda told me who else would be there when she hired me. I knew of Edward because of the restaurant he owned here in Southern California and because he had a reputation for being difficult, but I'd never met him. Christie's and Hugo's names didn't ring a bell and still don't."

"What about Brenda? Did you know of her before she hired you?"

"No, I'd never heard of her, either."

"You didn't watch the TV show *Premier Chef*?"

"I didn't even know it existed. I'm sorry I can't help more. Happy Valentine's Day."

I wished her well and hung up. I'd almost forgotten about Valentine's Day. Would I hear from Jason? Should I call him? Text him? Valentine's Day was bound to be busy at the restaurant despite its falling on a Monday this year, so I held off. He might get a second to call me.

Because I'd blocked off the day for the hotel event, I didn't have anything on my schedule. I did laundry and ordered baking ingredients from my supplier, then read my book.

Before I knew it, four o'clock had rolled around. The bulk of the day had passed without Jason contacting me. I texted him a heart emoji and said I hoped he wasn't too stressed. I didn't hear back. I went into the kitchen to bake four cherry meringue tarts for Tristan and Jeremy and left to deliver them.

As soon as I knocked on the door, Tristan answered, Jeremy standing behind him. They invited me in and I gave them the CliffsNotes version of the murder and what had happened since then. They were shocked and concerned but extended their wholehearted support and reassurance. Not wanting to impose on them any further on Valentine's Day, I came back home to whip up a few raspberry cream cupcakes for myself, which I ate by candlelight for dinner.

JASON TEXTED ME THE NEXT MORNING to wish me a late Happy Valentine's Day. I wrote back to thank him and then left to meet Isabella at the clubhouse restaurant. The community's gardening group had taken over most of the tables, so she was busy. She couldn't sit with me, but after delivering the group's order, she brought me a decaf cherry latte—a leftover Valentine's special—and said she could take a minute for chatting before checking in on them.

"Guess what?" she said, her long-lashed brown eyes lighting up. "Brian's Valentine's gift is a trip to Vegas. We're going later this week."

Because she had a penchant for jumping to conclusions when it came to her boyfriend, I warned her not to expect a quickie wedding. She laughed good-naturedly, and said they were only going to see a show and gamble a bit. She swore that a wedding hadn't crossed her mind.

I told her about my plan to attend Edward's memorial service on Thursday and Detective Hernandez's request to see me.

"That's the same day I go to Vegas. Otherwise, I'd go with. Could Jason go?"

"No. I asked him, but he has to work because Timothy's not going to be in that day."

She returned to the gardening group. Based on her harried expression, I guessed they would keep her hopping. Since I had some time, I took my coffee into the kitchen to talk to her boss, Vincent.

I'd recently learned of Vincent's lifelong dream to become a baker. He'd taken me up on my offer to give him lessons, and we'd had several since then. We hadn't been especially successful thus far, but I had high hopes we'd turn things around soon. I planned to check in on his chocolate cake homework and discuss his availability for learning pies.

He greeted me with a quick hug.

"Good timing. It's ready," he said, pointing to a large plate on the counter. "I think it came out pretty well." The cake was lopsided and poorly frosted, but sometimes good things came in not-so-attractive packages.

"Let's taste," I said.

He sliced off a piece and put it on a dish for me. I took a bite while he ran a hand across his bald head.

The cake was dense and dry with no redeeming features. "Not bad," I said, covering up my distaste with a smile. "I think you put in too much sugar, though. Remember to keep an eye on that."

His expression fell. This was the biggest drawback to being his teacher. Despite how carefully I framed my critiques, I always ended up hurting his feelings, and I hated that.

Scrambling to make him feel better, I said, "It's a good effort, Vincent. You're getting there. When do you want to have our pie lesson?"

"Friday at four?"

"That works for me. See you soon."

One nice side effect of teaching Vincent to bake was he didn't give Isabella a hard time anymore when she took a break with me. He apparently hadn't hassled her for requesting time off to go to Vegas, either. Another good side effect was the restaurant's standing order for me to provide desserts until Vincent was proficient enough to make them himself. Given how he was doing in our lessons, I'd probably be baking for him for some time.

I called my father Wednesday morning to tell him my plans for the following day.

"I was going to stay here in Napa a bit longer, but I could come down to Oceanville instead if you'd like some support," he said. "What if I set out today and book a hotel? We can meet up tomorrow and go together."

"Really? You don't have to get back to work?"

"Not yet. We can go in my rental car, if that's good for you."

"That would be great," I said. "I'll meet you at the hotel. Text me the information."

After hanging up with Dad, I checked my watch. Time for my long-scheduled meeting at Jan and Austin Williams's house to discuss the dessert for their anniversary party. I was feeling rather tired so decided to drive. I went outside and hopped in my mini-van.

Tristan and Jeremy were out on the driveway and flagged me down.

I rolled down the window. "Hey, guys."

With an uncharacteristic frown on his face, Tristan said, "Doll, some reporters were here sniffing around hoping to get a quote from you."

"Oh, no. What happened?"

"We told them you had nothing to do with the murder and to go away," Jeremy said. "They might be back. If you see them, let us know and we'll chase them off again."

"Thanks. I appreciate it a lot. I'm sorry you had to deal with them."

I turned onto Sea Lion Drive, remembering I hadn't given my friends possible dates for dinner. I'd have to do that soon. As for the reporters, I could only hope they would give up now. Dealing with the media was the last thing I wanted to do.

I stepped out of my mini-van at the Williams's house on Fish Lane and looked wistfully at my late friend Trudy's house next door. I'd heard that a new resident, a woman in her eighties, had moved in. I didn't feel up to it at the moment, but I made a mental note to bake her a batch of cookies as a housewarming gift.

I was anxious to meet with Jan and Austin as I had several ideas for the dessert they'd commissioned. My favorite design was a sheet cake with a surfing scene because the two had met while taking a lesson. They'd hit it off immediately and were inseparable from that point on. I was also fond of a round cake featuring penguins playing golf near a water hazard. I had a few thoughts for the fillings as well, including lemon and strawberry. Although it was fun to bake something different for The Countryside Inn event, I was looking forward to returning to my business's theme of ocean-themed creations. All my desserts were non-perishable, keeping in line with California's regulations for home-based bakeries.

Jan opened the door when I knocked and looked at me warily. "Kayla. You didn't get my email?"

I shook my head. "No, sorry. What's up? Are you okay?"

Jan shut the door behind her and came outside. "I'm afraid I have to cancel. We've decided to go with Icings for the dessert."

"But why?" Despite my query, I had a feeling I already knew.

"Well . . ."

"Please, just tell me."

"It's Austin. He's concerned. You were in the kitchen when that chef was killed. And last year, you found Trudy's and Stanley's bodies. You've been involved in a lot of murder cases."

"It's a coincidence. A really bad, really awful coincidence. I didn't kill anyone."

"I believe you, of course. But Austin is skeptical. And when he has his mind made up about something, it's impossible to change it."

Before I could process this, Marcus, Jan's youngest son, came around the corner on the lawn on all fours. He approached me and rubbed against my ankles.

"Um. Hi, Marcus," I said.

Jan explained, "He's a bunny in his school's annual spring production next month. But he's acting like a cat. Remember, honey, I told you that bunnies hop. And they screw up their noses." Jan demonstrated, looking like Samantha in *Bewitched*.

"They could change his part. He could be a kitten," I said. "Kittens are spring-like."

"I'll suggest it to the teacher. Thanks, Kayla. And I'm sorry."

I gave her the best smile I could muster and left.

ON THE WAY HOME, I DECIDED TO SWING BY the community offices on Otter Street to doublecheck my booking for the upcoming

Founder's Festival. The festival was a big deal in Seaside Shores. Each year on the anniversary of the grand opening on March 5th, 1980, we celebrated Theresa Alden, the founder of the community, with a 5K run and lunch. I'd been contributing the desserts since I'd moved to Seaside Shores, and I'd already decided to make mermaid sugar cookies and cupcakes with shark fins coming out the top. Ocean-themed and whimsical—perfect, I thought, for the family party.

The receptionist, Miranda, bit her lip when she saw me come in.

"Miranda, do not tell me they're cancelling on me."

She smiled guiltily. "Okay, I won't."

"But they are?"

"I'm afraid so," she said. "A couple of the board members kicked up a fuss over a murder suspect providing the desserts. They overruled the ones who supported you."

"I'm only a witness, not a suspect," I said, hoping that was true.

"I'm sorry, Kayla."

Sure, everyone was sorry. But sorrys didn't keep my business from collapsing. Maybe Dad had been right when we first met up at the hotel. I should have stayed in my customer service job. Or followed in his accountant footsteps and remained at the same firm for decades. If I had, I wouldn't be in this predicament. I'd never have been at The Countryside Inn, wouldn't have been in the kitchen at the time of Edward's murder, and my clients wouldn't be cancelling on me right and left.

Driving home to my cottage, I came up with all sorts of negative outcomes. What if I could no longer afford my rent? I knew Tristan would be sympathetic, but he hadn't been selling much of his art lately and he needed my rent money. I collected interest every month off an inheritance from my late grandmother, and I'd received some unexpected reward money the month before, so that would help. It wasn't enough to sustain me for long, however. If worse came to worst, my cats would eat and I would not, at least until I was able to land a job.

WHAT WITH THOUGHTS OF THE MURDER, worries about my numerous cancellations, and my conscience nagging at me for not telling Jason I'd decided to go forward with my plans the next day, I was too aware of one or the other cat leaving the bed and coming back throughout the night. Despite my thick drapes, light from the full moon filtered into the bedroom, making them restless. Flour at one point climbed onto my chest and lay down. While it was a sweet gesture, it did nothing to improve my sleep, as I had a hard time breathing with a solid twelve pounds on my chest—what both she and Sugar had weighed at their recent physicals. The vet hadn't said they were overweight but he'd implied they were getting there. I decided then and there that I would cut back on their food.

I woke up at six, fed the cats, and went back to bed until seven. After breakfast and my shower, I returned to the bedroom to put on my little black dress and black shoes, my go-to outfit for special events or, as in this case, memorials. After transferring essentials from my messenger bag to a small purse, I checked my emails. There was another cancellation, but also orders from Vincent and Jason. Thank goodness for them.

I acknowledged the latest cancellation, then texted Vincent and Jason to thank them for their orders, saying I'd make the deliveries on Saturday. Vincent responded with a smiley face and Jason wrote back to tell me to have a good day, not asking what I had planned. I sent him a reply to let him know I'd be out for the day, but I didn't hear back.

Promising I'd return in the late afternoon, I gave the cats a few spoonfuls of kitty tuna from a can, though less than I might have given my vow in the middle of the night. They ran to their plates and started inhaling food.

When I was ready to go, I locked the front door behind me and went outside to meet Isabella, who was driving me to meet my dad on her way to pick up Brian for Vegas. After I'd seen the steep parking fee for Dad's hotel, I'd asked if she'd drop me off.

As we drove past the road to the wharf, I said, "Remember when you first told Brian you loved him and he didn't say it back?"

"Of course. Not my finest moment."

"He's said it to you since then, hasn't he?"

She glanced over at me. "Yeah, we say it all the time. Why? Don't you and Jason?"

I had a feeling she would say that. A heavy feeling settled on my chest, similar to Flour lying on me in the middle of the night. "No. He said it in January but never again. And I've never told him."

"Whoa. Is that why you and he are struggling?"

"I think that's the root of it, yes. He's probably expecting me to say it."

"Well, okay, then." She reached into the console for her package of gum, unwrapped a piece, and stuck it into her mouth. She looked at me and gestured to the package, but I shook my head.

"Any sage advice?" I asked.

"If you don't feel it, you don't feel it."

I still didn't know for sure *what* I felt, and it was driving me nuts.

Isabella pulled into the drop-off zone at Dad's hotel a few minutes later. The hotel was inland from the water, and I guessed Dad had decided not to spring for an oceanfront property.

"Good luck," Isabella said as I opened the passenger door.

"Likewise." I grinned. "Don't do anything I wouldn't do."

"Then I guess I'll be staying in the hotel room with a book the entire time," Isabella responded, crossing her eyes at me.

"Ha, ha. Have a good time, Iz."

"See you, sweetie." She gave me a quick hug before I climbed out of the car, leaving her heady scent of gardenia perfume on my dress, and she drove off.

Dad met me in the lobby wearing a dark-grey suit with a maroon tie, his hair neatly combed. His glasses sat squarely on his nose. He must have used one of those tiny screwdrivers to tighten them.

"You look nice," I said.

"Thank you. As do you. How are your cats?"

I couldn't believe he was asking. "They're great. They missed me while I was gone at the hotel. I'm glad we'll be back later today."

"Assuming there aren't any murders," Dad said, laughing.

The very idea made my heart rate pick up. "Don't even joke about that."

He reached into his pocket and handed me a mini box of chocolates. He smiled at me shyly.

"A small Valentine's gift," he said. "Late, I know."

"Thanks, Dad. Chocolate is welcome anytime."

Dad led me to his rental car in the hotel garage. We drove to Los Robles, sharing the box of chocolates, and I told him about the reporters Tristan and Jeremy had scared off. We decided on a statement I could make in the future. I would say I was terribly sorry about Edward's death, but I had nothing to do with it, and I hoped his killer was caught soon.

"I've been getting cancellations," I said. "People don't want a possible killer as their baker. They're probably afraid I'll poison their dessert."

"That's terrible. We have to solve this." Dad's expression was determined, and he didn't even hint that I had chosen the wrong profession and should have stayed in my customer service job. My heart swelled. He did love me.

In Los Robles, we parked on the street in front of the police station, a building with stucco walls and a red tile roof, similar to The Countryside Inn. As I got out of the car, I saw Conrad Cunningham exiting the station holding a cup of what I assumed was coffee. His shirt was untucked and his hair looked like it hadn't been washed since the last time I'd seen him. The murder had obviously taken its toll on him.

I pointed him out to Dad. "It's Conrad, The Countryside's owner. We could ask him some questions."

"I'm game."

Dad and I approached. I hadn't noticed from farther away, but Conrad's shirt had a big stain on it. He was a mess.

"Conrad?" I said. "Are you okay?"

He looked at me, puzzled, seemingly not remembering me.

"Kayla Jeffries," I reminded him. "And this is my father, Andrew."

"Of course. Kayla, I apologize for not recognizing you. I've got a lot on my mind."

"Is something wrong?" I asked, cringing as soon as I said it. Of course something was wrong. There had been a murder at his hotel. "Something more, I mean?"

"The hotel is struggling," he said. "Ever since the news of the murder made it into the media, we've been getting cancellations and we've had no new bookings. The police haven't arrested anyone yet. As if that weren't enough, a few of the guests who were there that night are preparing a class action lawsuit. They're claiming emotional distress. I don't know if they have a case, but the publicity will be bad."

"I'm so sorry," I said. I looked to Dad, and he nodded at me to go ahead. "Is it all right if we ask you a few questions? I want to know who killed Edward and clear my name."

"I suppose so."

"I was late getting to the hotel the day Edward was killed. Did the other three chefs arrive separately or together? On time? Is there anything you can remember?"

"I've gone over all of this with the police. Christie and Edward showed up fifteen minutes apart, Edward arriving first. Hugo had only just gotten to the hotel when you arrived. He was also late."

"Is there anything you can tell us about the three?" Dad asked.

"They all applied to our open call for guest chefs. Edward owns—owned—a successful restaurant in Southern California. Christie had a restaurant, too, but it was sidelined by bad reviews. She had to close it. We hired her anyway. Bad reviews happen."

Hmm. Interesting. "And Hugo?"

"He's a local. He works at a restaurant in Greenbrook. We like to have at least one local cook for each guest chef weekend."

"How did you happen to hire Brenda as the kitchen manager?" I asked next.

Conrad shrugged. "She applied for the job a few months back. Our old manager had just left."

"Did you know she'd been on *Premier Chef* and won?" Dad said.

"She mentioned that. It's largely why I hired her. It's a line we use in our PR materials."

I thought for a minute. "It's her job to hire the guest chefs?"

"Yes. She goes through the applications first and makes her choices. I give the okay after that." He paused. "I suppose I should be talking about this in the past tense. It looks like that's all over now. *Everything* might be over now." He stared into his Styrofoam cup as if hoping he'd find answers there.

I filed away the information about the hiring.

Dad asked, "Do you have any theories on who killed Edward?"

"No, I don't. I'm sorry to cut this off, but I'd like to get going."

"Are you headed over to the service?" I asked.

"Yes."

"We'll see you soon, then."

DAD AND I WENT INSIDE THE POLICE STATION. "I'll be right here when you're done, K-Bear," Dad said.

I gave my name at the desk, showing my ID when requested. The officer picked up the phone to alert Det. Hernandez I was there, got the okay, buzzed me through the security door, and pointed to her right.

"Room 103," she said.

The door was open. I knocked on it anyway and Det. Hernandez motioned for me to come in.

"Ms. Jeffries, hello. Thank you for coming. Please sit down." I took a chair. "I have a couple of items to discuss."

"Okay," I said. "I'm ready."

"There was activity in the kitchen prior to the murder that you didn't report," he began. "Christie and Hugo both said there was bickering among the four chefs before dinner service." He rifled through some papers on his desk. "I have your statement right here." He made a point of looking it over. "Don't see anything about that."

"Oh," I said, unable to come up with an explanation.

"Might there be anything else you left out?" he asked.

"No. There's nothing else." I hoped that was true, but I'd been pretty shaken during our interview. I took a deep breath to steady my nerves. "I apologize for leaving that out. I have some information for you, too, if you're done with your questions."

"Oh, yes?"

"Edward and Brenda competed against each other on the first season of the reality show *Premier Chef*. It was a big deal. A nationally-televised show with good prize money, and chefs tend to be competitive with one another."

"And?"

"I think it means something," I said.

Det. Hernandez leaned back in his chair. "Ms. Jeffries, what makes you think this is new information for us?"

"It's . . . not?"

"No. Brenda Clarkson told us immediately about her relationship to the deceased. She was quite forthcoming about it. We would have found out anyway, you know."

"She could have had a professional grudge with him," I said.

"What kind of a grudge? She won the competition. He didn't."

I couldn't argue with that, but I wasn't ready to give up. "What if Edward was mad he hadn't won, said something inflammatory to Brenda, and she took the power outage as an opportunity to kill him in retaliation?"

"Did you witness such a statement?"

"Um, no. But it could have happened earlier in the day. Before I arrived."

"Conrad has accounted for Edward's whereabouts after he got to the hotel. He took Edward personally to check in with Brenda, and then on a tour. They had a snack together and Conrad escorted him back to the kitchen afterward. Conrad said nothing unusual happened during that time."

I gathered my thoughts and said, "Then I think it's possible, given all the hubbub in the kitchen, that something happened without my knowledge during dinner service. If Brenda and Edward were alone together in a corner, for example. And if they didn't raise their voices too much."

"Anything *could* have happened, Ms. Jeffries, but that's a lot of what-ifs."

"Well, what about Christie Nelson?" I asked. "It's my understanding she and Edward had a romantic relationship."

"Yes. Again, not new information."

I shook my head in frustration. "Detective, my reputation is on the line here. I've been getting cancellations for my business. Are they suspects, at least? I shouldn't be. They knew Edward. I didn't, like I told you."

He locked eyes with me. "And you're sure about that?"

What was he talking about? "Of course I'm sure about that. What do you mean?"

"I have credible information that contradicts that assertion."

"*What?* Did someone say I knew him?"

"I'm sorry. I'm unable to release that information."

We looked at each other, neither of us willing to budge.

"You can be on your way, Ms. Jeffries," the detective said to conclude the conversation. "We'll contact you if—and when—we want to speak with you again. Or, if you'd like to amend anything you've told me, give me a call." He took a business card from a holder on his desk and handed it to me.

I took the card reluctantly and left to return to Dad.

CHAPTER 6

D AD AND I DECIDED TO WALK TO THE SERVICE, as it was only a half mile away from the Los Robles police station in the adjacent city of La Tierra. I was wearing my black ballet flats, having sacrificed added inches to my 5'2" height in favor of comfort, so my shoes wouldn't be an issue. We left the station and started out. While we walked, I gave Dad the rundown on what had happened with the detective.

I kicked a small rock as far as I could, sending it rolling down the sidewalk. "I can't get over Detective Hernandez believing I knew Edward before the weekend. Do you think one of the others made that up and told him?"

Dad put his arm around my shoulder. "I don't know, honey. You're sure you'd never met Edward?"

"Yes, pretty sure, although now I'm having my doubts. The detective was so certain I knew him."

"Could you have met him socially?"

I laughed. "I'm an introvert. I try hard *not* to do social things."

Dad smiled. "What about at a job?"

I shook my head. "I worked in customer service right out of college. I've never been in the food industry. Outside my own home, I mean."

Dad thought for a few seconds. "When you were researching at the hotel, did you look up where Edward went to college?"

"No. I was more focused on the others than on him." I pulled my phone from my purse and ran a search. I found what I was looking for and gulped. "Uh, oh."

"What?" Dad asked. "Did you find out where he attended college?"

"He went to UC Springvale the same years I did. I don't remember an Edward Winthrop, though. But you know how big the school is."

"Perhaps he used a nickname in college. Ed? Eddie? Ted?"

I stopped walking.

Dad said, "Did you remember something?"

I nodded slowly as we started up again. "I took a literature class with someone named Ted. He was a constant mansplainer even though that word hadn't entered the lexicon yet. His last name *might* have been Winthrop." I tried to summon more information from my memory and failed. "I just don't know."

"That could be him."

"If so, I had hardly any contact with him, Dad. I might have exchanged a brief sentence with him once or twice. I certainly didn't recognize him all these years later. And *he* didn't recognize *me*, either, as far as I could tell."

"The police probably uncovered the fact that you and Edward went to UC Springvale at the same time, maybe even that you were in a class together. Detective Hernandez and company are most likely digging to see if they can find a deeper relationship. They could be trying to discover if you dated him and things went badly. The theory might be that when you saw him at the hotel, all the contentious feelings came back and you took the chance during the power outage to kill him."

"Well, they'll find nothing there. *If* we had that class together, I barely talked to him, let alone dated him."

"I'm sure that will all become clear."

We'd reached the rock and I kicked it again. I tried to calm myself by looking at the clusters of daffodils along our route and by thinking about my cats. We passed into La Tierra city limits and took a right on Serra Street.

I broke the silence first. "I don't want to let go of Brenda as a possible suspect yet. But, like Detective Hernandez said, *she* won the competition, not Edward. And no one saw them argue."

"Yes, that must be why the detective isn't considering her."

"Okay, but what if Edward had something on Brenda that nullified her win and she had to get rid of him so he wouldn't release the information? She could have seen his application and hired him for that purpose."

"We have to remember that the murder wasn't premeditated, K-Bear. No one could have known the power would go out from the wind. If Brenda had found out Edward could nullify her win and she'd decided to kill him at the hotel, wouldn't there have been a plan?"

"That's true."

"And what would he have that disqualified her?"

"I don't know. But you're right, killing someone with a nearby kitchen tool wasn't a planned act. Something must have triggered the murderer to do it. There *was* bickering as we were getting everything ready but nothing that could lead to murder. Whether there was anything later, I don't have any facts, like Detective Hernandez said."

The hairs on the back of my neck stood up and I whipped my head around. None other than Det. Hernandez was behind us.

"Are you following us, Detective?" I asked.

"Yes and no. As you can see, I'm definitely behind you, so in that sense I *am* following you. But it's only because I believe we're going to the same place." He gestured to a Spanish-style home to our left. I checked the house number and saw it was the address for the service. I supposed he was doing the same as we were—taking the opportunity to talk to people. Darn. Would that prevent *us* from talking to anyone?

The door was ajar. Det. Hernandez gestured for us to enter the house first, and Dad and I, exchanging a glance, went through.

A tall woman with her blond hair tied back in a bun introduced herself as Edward's Aunt Sally. We gave her our condolences, and she ushered the three of us outside to the backyard. Looking at the white folding chairs set up in neat rows, the bountiful flower arrangements, and the guests dressed in their finest, I couldn't help but think of the parallels to a wedding. The brilliant February day added to the effect. Under different circumstances, Edward's parents might have seen him get married today, in this very place. I felt a tug at my heartstrings. Edward had had his whole life ahead of him: career, spouse, children . . . and someone took all that away.

By unspoken agreement, Dad and I made sure we were nowhere near the detective. We settled ourselves in a back row while Det. Hernandez chose a seat to the side near the front. I waved at Conrad, who'd seated himself in the middle. He tried for a smile, but it came off looking more like a grimace.

A woman in her sixties, face pale and tendrils of hair escaping her updo, approached the podium in front of the rows of seats. I guessed this was Melody, Edward's mother.

She looked out at us, her face twisted in pain. Taking a deep breath, she said, "Welcome, everyone. Thank you for coming." She paused and gazed up at the sky before continuing. "When Edward was young, he rejected everything his father and I served him. He didn't want chicken fingers, hamburgers, or macaroni and cheese. Can you imagine? What child doesn't like macaroni and cheese?" A few light chuckles floated up from the audience. "But that was Edward. He began experimenting in the kitchen, trying to find something he wanted to eat. When he was only eight, he entered a BLT chili in the county fair. He won, hands-down. From then on, he did all the cooking. It was the best thing that ever happened to me." This was met with loud laughter and she smiled.

"All he wanted to do with his life was cook. But his father and I didn't think he could make a living being a chef. We encouraged him to get a degree in engineering when he went away to college."

Edward couldn't stay away from cooking for long, Melody went on, and he eventually went to culinary school and then mentored under popular chef Davinia Clarke. He opened his own restaurant in Los Angeles, which he named Spatula. The restaurant took off, and he was asked to join the first season of *Premier Chef.*

"He was a wonderful chef and a wonderful son, my Ted."

I nudged Dad in the shoulder when Melody used the nickname.

"I miss him so much. I don't know how I'll live without him," she ended, brushing tears from her eyes. I dug a tissue from my purse and dealt with my own tears.

"You okay, honey?" Dad whispered. I nodded.

Edward's Uncle Thomas and Aunt Sally spoke after Melody.

As Aunt Sally spoke, I looked around the backyard. I counted only twenty mourners spread out through the ten rows, including Dad and myself. None of our possible suspects was present. I didn't recognize anyone besides Conrad and Det. Hernandez. I saw no well-known chefs nor any of the *Premier Chef* contestants. Were all those Facebook condolences just for show? No one bothered to make the trip, as much as they loved and admired Edward and were devastated by his untimely death?

At the end of the service, I watched Conrad slip out the back gate. He likely had to get back to the hotel. Dad and I stood and went into the house.

The home was decorated for visual effect and not comfort. The furniture, while beautiful, didn't look relaxing to sit in. It was all angles and scratchy-looking fabric. Large abstract paintings covered the walls, making me even more grateful for Tristan's soothing scene above my fireplace. The sounds of smooth jazz streamed throughout the house, and I wondered if it had been Edward's favorite kind of music.

I nibbled on vegetables and dip as I pondered whom to talk to. Right when I decided to speak with Thomas, who'd said in his eulogy that he and his nephew had been close, Det. Hernandez was already there. When I finally caught sight of Melody again, the detective was talking with *her.* I crisscrossed the living room floor countless times, but Det. Hernandez was always one step ahead. What the heck? I eventually gave up, and Dad and I left.

ON THE WALK BACK TO OUR CAR at the police station, Dad said, "I didn't learn anything, did you?"

"No, not a thing. I thought either Melody or the uncle might have known more about Edward's relationship with Christie and who broke up with whom, or they might have the scoop about *Premier Chef* and whether there was animosity between him and Brenda because of it. But Detective Hernandez was always there. I didn't even get to tell Melody how sorry I am."

"I had the same experience. It's like the detective was in five places at once."

We were silent for a few beats as we considered our next steps. I wanted nothing more than to have my name cleared so I could go back to baking, walking on the coastal path, and working things out with Jason. Perhaps I needed to talk to my suspects directly.

"What now, Miss Marple?" Dad asked.

Before I could answer, Detective Hernandez passed by on the other side of the street. He was walking faster than we were and soon outdistanced us.

My eyes on his retreating form, I said, "I think I'd better tell Detective Hernandez I knew Edward in college, but as Ted."

"Good idea."

THE POLICE OFFICER AT THE DESK got permission for us to see Det. Hernandez and she buzzed us in. We headed for the detective's office, where he was taking off his coat and hanging it up.

"Hello again," he said. "Remember something?"

I formally introduced Dad and said, "Yes. I've just realized I was in a college class with Edward, but he was going by Ted then. I didn't know him. I barely even talked to him."

"Thank you for clearing that up. Anything else to share?"

"No, that's it."

He nodded at us and we left.

"Do you think he believed me?" I asked Dad as we walked toward the car.

"I hope so. He keeps his cards close to his chest." That was for sure. I wished Det. Hernandez had told me I had nothing to worry about and was certainly not a suspect. Talking to him hadn't gone off as I'd planned, nor had the memorial service.

I ached to accomplish *something* on this trip. I said to Dad, "When I was searching for Hugo on the internet, I came up with an address in Greenbrook, which is only a couple of towns over."

"What are you thinking?" he asked.

"We could go and talk to him. I'd like to ask if he knew Edward. There was no link between the two that I could find."

"I didn't find anything, either."

"I don't think the detour will delay us much getting back to Oceanville," I said.

"I'm in."

"I'm so glad you're with me, Dad. Your superhero accountant skills are helping and I appreciate the support."

"There's nowhere I'd rather be."

I verified Hugo's address and got directions to his house. We ran into a bit of traffic but made it there in fifteen minutes.

Hugo was pushing his legs back and forth on the porch swing when we arrived at his ranch-style home. He waved at us enthusiastically, apparently unperturbed or even surprised that we'd tracked him down. A cowlick in the front of his hair, which I hadn't noticed when we were together at the hotel, was sticking up, making him look like a little boy.

"Hi, Hugo," I said. "Nice to see you again. This is my dad, Andrew."

"Great to meet you. Have a seat." He scooted over. He didn't seem to remember Dad from the café on the night of the murder.

Dad and I sat on the swing and awkwardly pumped our legs in time with Hugo. There was not a lot of room for the three of us, and Hugo was so close to me that I picked up his scents of soap and shampoo. A camellia bush overflowing with blossoms was in my line of vision, so I concentrated on that rather than on his smells and the fact that his arm was brushing against mine.

"What brings you folks to Greenbrook?" Hugo asked.

"Well, we've been at Edward's memorial service in La Tierra

and thought we'd come see you. I just wanted to talk to you about a couple of things," I said.

"Sure. What's up?"

"I don't know about you, but I don't like being on the news in association with a murder case. I've been getting cancellations for my business. Has your job been affected?"

"No, I've still got it. My boss is cool."

"That's good," I said. "Do you have any theories on who might have killed Edward? Do you know if anyone had a motive?"

He stopped swinging and leaned forward, looking like a misbehaving child who had stolen and eaten all the chocolate chip cookies. The unruly cowlick added to the effect. "Dude, I was lucky. I had a possible motive, but the police didn't find out."

Dad and I looked at each other behind Hugo's back. Dad raised his eyebrows at me.

"Really? How did you know Edward? What motive?" I asked.

"I worked for him for about five weeks at his restaurant a couple of years ago. He fired me. I might have wanted to get back at him because of that."

"And did you?" Dad asked.

Hugo didn't seem at all fazed by the question. "Nah. He was an arrogant you-know-what, but I wouldn't kill him."

"What about Christie?" I asked. I looked at Dad. "I heard a rumor they'd been involved once."

"Oh, sure. It was big news in the cooking world. They were hot and heavy, though they did the breaking up and getting back together thing all the time. Edward broke up with her for good after he got runner-up on *Premier Chef.* He thought she was beneath him. Man, that was cold."

I wasn't getting a very pleasant picture of Edward, but he didn't deserve to be stabbed in the back of the neck.

"It's a drag," Hugo said. "I was hoping to impress Conrad enough so he'd hire me on full-time. The word on the street is they're about to lose one of their permanent chefs. I'm a line cook for the restaurant where I'm at now, but I want to earn more money. I'd like to move away from the parental unit." He gestured backward to his house.

"I'm sorry the hotel didn't work out," I said.

"Thanks. Do the cops have anything on you?"

"They might think they do, because I was in a class with Edward in college. But I didn't know him."

Hugo nodded and bent to tie his shoelace.

"Now that The Countryside Inn isn't an option for you, what are you going to do?" Dad asked.

"I'm hoping Christie can hook me up. She also wanted the permanent gig at The Countryside. She said she was gonna go back to a restaurant in San Francisco she worked at before she opened her own. See if they'd hire her again. I asked her to put in a good word for me."

"What's the restaurant called? I might want to talk to her," I said.

"Balsamic. Hey, do you guys want some hand pies? I just made up a batch."

"Sure," I said at the same time Dad answered, "Love some."

We all got up and Hugo tripped. Dad put out his hand to help him regain his balance.

"I'm a total klutz," Hugo told us. He led us inside to the kitchen where two baking sheets of hand pies sat on the counter. He found a paper bag in a drawer and opened it up.

"These ones are ground beef and potato," he said, turning to one of the baking sheets. After dropping two pies on the floor and tossing them into the sink, he filled the bag halfway. He then took several pies from the other baking sheet and stuffed the bag to the top. "These guys are strawberry."

We thanked him. I hadn't had any food at the memorial service other than veggies and dip, and I didn't think Dad had, either.

"What's your take?" Dad asked after we'd bid Hugo good-bye and were in the car on our way back to Oceanville. He took a bite of his ground beef and potato pie, careful to keep his eyes on the road.

"I don't think Hugo did it. I hope he can put this behind him and get a new job." I chomped on my own pie. "Oh, my gosh. This is fantastic. Jason would love these. I wonder if I'd be able to create my own recipe."

"They're quite good," Dad agreed.

"Dad, despite what Hugo said, I bet the police found out Edward fired him. If I were to tell Detective Hernandez, he'd probably say it's not new information."

"Yes. Hugo struck me as a tad naïve."

"I think so too. What about this potential opening for a permanent chef? Hugo said he and Christie both wanted it. Do you think there's anything there?"

"Wouldn't one of them be dead, then, and not Edward?"

"Good thinking. Edward wouldn't have been trying for the position. He already had his own restaurant and a successful one at that."

"Right. I don't think that's it, K-Bear. Any other thoughts?"

"I think I'm gonna go up to the Bay Area to find Christie at Balsamic. I'd like to ask her about her relationship with Edward." I took another bite of pie.

"Shall I go with you? I could take a few more days. I'll hold onto my hotel room in Oceanville."

"Yeah? That'd be great." I never would have described my dad as spontaneous. He'd always been a man with a plan.

I checked my calendar on my phone and saw I had work to do. I had Jason's and Vincent's orders to fulfill and was surprised to see a personal event scheduled for the next night, Friday. I'd forgotten that Jason and I had a longstanding date to see his sister, Paula, for her February 18th birthday. She had invited us for homemade pasta and salad a while ago and I'd said I'd make the cake.

"What about Tuesday?" I asked Dad. "Or is that too far away? Do you have to go back home sooner?"

"No, that'll work out well. I can do a little sightseeing until then. Or get some sun at the beach." He chuckled at my astonished expression. I'd never known him to sunbathe. Yep, he was a different person for sure.

"It's a date," I said. "Do you mind if I make a phone call?"

"Not at all."

Jason answered after a couple of rings. "Hey," he said. The clamor of the kitchen in the background was rather pleasant until what sounded like a stack of plates crashed to the floor.

"Sorry about that," he said. "Everyone's clumsy today. Mercury must be in retrograde or something."

"Mercury," I repeated. "Right."

"So, hi," he said.

"Hi. How are you?"

"Fine. How are you?"

"Fine." This reminded me of my initial meeting with my dad, all this empty talk and nothingness. "So, listen. We're supposed to go to Paula's tomorrow night, but I understand, well, if you don't want me there."

My statement was met with such a long pause that I thought he'd hung up.

Finally, he said, "It's up to you, but it would be nice if you came with me."

Whether he meant nice for him or for Paula, I didn't know.

"Great," I said, with too much over-the-top enthusiasm. "I'll make the cake tomorrow morning."

I hung up and groaned. Dad looked at me curiously.

I didn't feel like getting into my issues with Jason again, so I said, "Should we try the desserts?" I rummaged through the paper bag and came up with two strawberry pies. I handed one to Dad and took a big bite of my own. The dessert was fresh and bright, the sweet strawberries the perfect contrast to the almost savory crust. Incredible.

Back in Oceanville, I directed Dad to my cottage in Seaside Shores. I promised to invite him over soon so he could meet the cats and have a tour. I explained I was too exhausted at the moment to have company and would like some quiet time. He said he understood. I kissed him on the cheek before exiting the car, glad we were having a chance to get to know each other again.

I SLEPT LATE, TIRED FROM THE EVENTS of the day before. After breakfast, I spent the rest of the morning baking and decorating Paula's birthday cake. I made and ate a sandwich, then got started on Vincent's and Jason's orders. The work, equal parts creative and precise, soothed my rattled nervous system. Before I knew it, I was due at the clubhouse restaurant for Vincent's next baking lesson.

This time, a towel caught fire on the stove and Vincent oversalted his pie crust to the point it was inedible. I did my best to reassure him and went home to get ready for Paula's birthday dinner.

Jason picked me up at six. He helped me secure my cake in the back seat and we took off.

"What were you up to yesterday?" he asked. "Your text was a little vague. Did you end up going to the memorial service?"

"I did. My dad went with me."

"Your dad? You mean your stepfather?"

"Oh, I guess I didn't get to tell you. My dad is in the area. He was actually at the hotel when the murder happened."

"Really?" Jason said, turning to give me a quick look. "That's coincidental."

"Not really. My mom told him I'd be at the hotel and he came to see me on his way to visit a friend in Napa. We've been spending time together. It's been nice."

"I'm glad to hear that. I remember you saying the two of you haven't always gotten along."

"True," I said. "But we've been talking a lot and understanding each other better. He's helping me get through the aftermath of the murder. And so he went with me yesterday."

"I'm sure the victim's family appreciated you going to pay your respects. That's all you did, right?"

"Right," I answered, my voice cracking. I knew I was straddling the line of dishonesty if not brazenly crossing it. I hadn't talked to anyone at the service about the murder but I'd intended to.

"Good."

"We also went to the police station," I said. "The lead detective, David Hernandez, asked me to stop by to clear up a few things."

"What kinds of things?"

"I didn't realize it at first, but Edward and I went to UC Springvale at the same time. We had a class together. He was going by Ted then. I hope the detective believed me when I told him I had virtually no contact with Edward in the class and didn't recognize him at the hotel."

"I'm sure he believed you. That's it, then? You're done?"

"I don't know if he'll have more questions for me, but I've got to get him to focus on the others who were there when Edward was murdered. More cancellations have been coming in. Big ones. I'm worried my business is about to collapse."

"We've talked about this, Kayla. I understand your concerns, but I'm concerned too. I wish you'd stay out of it."

We were quiet after that. Fortunately, Paula lived in Seaside Shores only a few blocks from my cottage, so the drive was short. We parked at the curb and got out of the car.

In keeping with the community's color schemes, Paula's house was painted dark green with mint accents. We took the steps up to the porch, passing by several fish and dolphin garden statues.

Paula swung open the door. She greeted us warmly, we wished her a happy birthday, and she took us inside.

"Perfect timing. Dinner's ready," she said. She invited us to sit at the dining room table while she brought in the food, declining our offers to help. We dug into the Caesar salad and pasta with pesto sauce. Everything was amazing, but Jason and I kept stumbling over ourselves whenever we spoke.

"Do you want more salad, Jason?" I asked at the same time he said, "Kayla, would you like more bread?"

"Yes," I said as he answered, "No, thank you."

"Sorry," we both said, looking sheepishly at Paula. She rolled her eyes at us. I had a feeling I'd hear about this later.

Sure enough, when I helped her wash the dishes after dinner, she said, "Everything okay with you guys?"

I didn't want to upset Paula on her birthday. Deciding not to get into the whole "I love him/I love him not" dilemma, I said, "He's worried about my involvement in another murder investigation. I understand why he's bothered, but I have to clear my name. I've been losing business."

"He told me about that. Makes sense to me that you'd want to protect yourself and your livelihood." Paula, a fellow HSP, was always quick to understand how other people felt.

"Thanks. That means a lot."

"Listen, Kayla, you two are good together. I've never seen him so happy as when he's with you. I know you'll figure it out."

"I appreciate your faith in us." I handed her the last dish to dry. "I have a surprise for you. I'll be right back."

I got the keys from Jason, went outside to the car, and grabbed my domed cake plate from the backseat.

Paula made decaf lattes and we gathered at the coffee table, settling onto the plush blue carpet. Paula's black Lab, Midnight, sat next to me, hoping something tasty was in the offing, and I fondled her ears before removing the dome. I revealed the cake I'd made in the shape of a turtle and yelled, "Ta da!"

"It's beautiful, Kayla," Paula said, touching my shoulder. She tucked her dark brown hair behind her ears and admired the dessert.

"Not only is it shaped like a turtle but that's the flavor too. Chocolate, caramel, and pecans. It's a turtle cake on two levels." I grinned.

"That's amazing. How did you make the body?" Paula asked.

"I have a special dome cake pan. I used fondant for the head and flippers. You probably don't want to eat that part. A lot of people don't like the taste of fondant."

"Well, it's incredible," she said.

"This is really something, honey." Jason gave me a peck on the cheek. I couldn't remember the last time he'd kissed me. If I knew it was as easy as making a cake, I would have done it sooner.

Paula took a picture with her phone before I cut into the turtle and passed out slices. Both Jason and Paula raved over the cake and requested seconds.

When we'd agreed we were all stuffed and couldn't eat another bite, Jason said, "Ready for presents?"

"You know me, big brother," Paula said. "I'm always ready for presents."

Jason gave her a weighted blanket like the one he'd given me for Christmas. She exclaimed over it and laid it across her lap. I told her how much I liked mine and she became even more enthusiastic. She opened my gift, a pair of blue dangly earrings, and put them on right away.

Before Jason and I left, we played three games of Scrabble, each of us winning a round. Paula sent us away with leftover pasta and cake, thanking us for a wonderful evening. I'd had a great time too. It was such a pleasure to spend time with two of my favorite people after the week I'd had.

CHAPTER 7

O N THE DRIVE HOME AFTER OUR DINNER with Paula, Jason glanced over at me and said, "I've been thinking we should go somewhere. Have time away from work and chores and regular life. Just the two of us."

My breath caught. This was the first time he'd suggested a getaway. Although he'd taken time off here and there and we'd spent a number of days living together in December, we'd never gone out of town. I'd had daydreams of us sharing a leisurely weekend of delicious dinners, long walks, and sleeping late. It could be exactly what we needed. The murder investigation would be there when we got back—or, if I were lucky, the police would have solved the crime by then or Dad and I would crack the case after talking with Christie.

Plus, if I were going to tell Jason I loved him, what better time than when we were focused on only each other with a beautiful locale as our backdrop? The following weekend would be perfect.

"That sounds—" I started.

"What about leaving this Monday and coming back Wednesday?" he broke in. "We could go up to Lake Tahoe. Stop by your parents' in Springvale on the way if you think it's the right time for me to meet them. Timothy can handle the restaurant."

Uh, oh. Dad and I already had plans to go see Christie.

"I'm afraid I can't. I'm doing something on Tuesday." To avoid looking at him, I opened the glove compartment and peered inside. I pored over the car registration like it was a newly-found novel by a Brontë sister.

"Do you have a booking?" he asked. "A wedding? A party?"

"No. Nothing like that."

"Then what?"

I pulled a map out of the glove compartment and held it up to him. "Old school."

"Kayla, would you please tell me what you're doing on Tuesday? I'm starting to feel a little insecure."

"Dad and I are going to San Francisco."

"San Francisco? Why? Not investigating, I hope."

"Well . . . yes. I'd like to talk to Christie, one of the other chefs. I have a lead that she might be working at a restaurant there. She had a romantic relationship with the victim. She may have killed him."

His jaw was tight with worry.

"My dad will be with me," I said. "Nothing bad will happen."

Jason turned into my driveway and drew up in front of my house. We looked at each other expectantly.

"Thanks for driving," I said. "I'll keep you posted."

"Good. Thank you for coming."

I attempted to kiss his cheek, but he tilted his head to a sound on the driveway and I got his ear instead. Embarrassed, I exited the car and went inside.

Just as I was getting ready for bed, my phone chimed and my heart pitter-pattered. Could it be Jason suggesting a different getaway date? Nope. Not Jason, but one of my clients. I opened the email and found yet another cancellation. I frowned and sent a reply, saying I was sorry to hear it but looked forward to working with her in the future.

It took me forever to get to sleep. I felt overwhelmed by the as-small-as-it-was party at Paula's, the cancellations that threatened to sink my business, my flailing relationship with Jason, and, of course, the murder of a fellow chef. I couldn't believe it hadn't even been a week since Edward had been killed. Now that I was thinking about it, every time I closed my eyes, the sight of his body on the kitchen floor flashed in front of me. I tossed and turned my way through the night.

THE HOT AND WINDY WEATHER had given way to pleasant days with a few puffy clouds in the sky. I decided on a new routine of taking the cats on supervised excursions out to the back patio. They were tiring of their myriad of toys and sometimes followed me around bellowing as if expecting me to entertain them.

The day after Paula's party, I retrieved the cozy mystery I was reading, put on my clip-on sunglasses, and called for the cats. They came running and tore out the sliding glass door ahead of me, practically tripping me in the process.

The back area of my cottage was mostly concrete patio with a couple of patches of dirt and a few trees, all surrounded by a short fence. The space wouldn't be on Seaside Shores's garden tour anytime soon, but I enjoyed sitting out there when the weather wasn't too hot or too cold.

As I read on the plastic chaise longue I'd set up to catch the sun, the cats watched birds fly from tree to tree and waited for lizards to appear.

After a few minutes, Sugar ran over to me, triumphantly holding a lizard in her mouth. I praised her, took the reptile from her, and got up to place it on the other side of the fence. She looked up at me, dumbfounded. Then she went back to trying to find one and I returned to the chaise.

Flour circled the chaise, alternately watching Sugar and giving me doe eyes, apparently wanting reassurance for her lack of hunting ability. She jumped up next to me and I scratched her back.

"You have other talents," I told her. "We've got to go in for now. I have to bake."

The two obliged quite readily when I led them inside, but I worried it wouldn't always be so easy.

That afternoon, after a long day of baking, I delivered an order of dolphin-shaped sugar cookies to a five-year-old's birthday party, fittingly hosted at a house on Porpoise Lane. The kids showed their delight with the cookies by making the dolphins "swim" through the air, and I found the experience rewarding, if noisy.

I drove back home to load Vincent's and Jason's orders into the mini-van and left to deliver them.

Stopping by the clubhouse restaurant first, I entered the lobby, waved to Isabella, and went into the kitchen. Vincent looked a little hangdog, no doubt from the ill-fated lesson the day before, so I told him to give it another try and I'd return the next day for a tasting. He thanked me for the vanilla and chocolate cakes I'd brought and gave me a check.

When I arrived at Fishes Do Come True with the chocolate cakes and apple pies Jason had asked for, the hostess said he was cooking and couldn't come out.

"He's swamped," she said. "Leave them here with me. Can you send an invoice?"

"I can take them to him in the kitchen," I said, trying to balance the four bakery boxes in my arms without dropping them. "It's no problem."

"I'm sorry. He said he doesn't want to be disturbed." She looked down at the reservation sheet and picked up the phone.

"Okay. Tell him thanks for me." I stacked the boxes on the hostess stand, returned to the delivery parking lot, and drove back to the cottage.

Once home, distressed that I hadn't seen Jason, I collapsed onto the bed and held Flour close to my chest. I lay there quietly with my eyes shut. Flour loved it, but after a while, I had the urge to do something productive. First, I emailed an invoice to Jason. Then, wanting to make a dent in the murder case, I decided to reprise my investigative aid from the year before of using a logic grid to keep track of suspects and motives.

I retrieved a piece of printer paper and a pencil from my office and headed for the living room. Sitting on the floor at the coffee table, I wrote "MOTIVES" at the top of the paper, and along the side, I listed Brenda's, Hugo's, and Christie's names.

I drew a grid and looked over my handiwork. According to the grid, this investigation was simpler than my first. Last time, I'd had a number of possibilities for whodunit. Now, there were only a certain few who could have murdered Edward. Plus, I didn't need columns for "MEANS" and "OPPORTUNITY." All of the suspects had the opportunity and the physical ability to kill Edward with the shears. The grid looked awfully empty so I decided to add my own customized column, titled "REASONS AGAINST."

I twirled the pencil around in my fingers as I considered the three suspects and their motives. I started with Hugo, who might have exacted revenge because Edward fired him. I wrote "firing?" under the "Motive" heading. In the "Reasons Against" column, I penciled in "too naïve?"

As for Brenda, she may have killed Edward because of some professional beef related to the reality show they'd competed on together. I wrote "*Premier Chef*?" under "Motive," but hurried to add "she won the competition" under "Reasons Against."

I moved on to Christie. Perhaps her tempestuous relationship with Edward had led her to kill him. I remembered Hugo saying Edward thought he was too good for her. I decided on "relationship?" for the motive. I hadn't talked to her yet, so I left the "Reasons Against" column blank.

There were too many question marks and nothing solid. I was no closer to knowing who the murderer was. Putting away the grid, I jotted down questions for Christie. She might turn out to be the killer, my name would be cleared, and life would return to normal.

THE NEXT MORNING, I STOPPED BY TO SEE VINCENT AGAIN. This time, he'd baked a lemon meringue pie. The filling was sour, the meringue flat, and the pie crust burnt. I struggled to find something positive to say.

"The crust isn't salty this time," I said. "Good job on that. Why don't you give it one more try?"

He agreed. There wasn't much else to say, so I went back home.

ISABELLA, NEWLY BACK FROM LAS VEGAS, invited me to have lunch with her at the clubhouse restaurant on Monday during her break. We settled in to eat crab sandwiches and fries.

"We had a great time," she said, her face aglow. "We won two hundred and seventeen dollars. The show was fun. And we got some good deals."

"That's terrific, Iz." I brought her up-to-date on what had been happening on my end. "I've been getting more cancellations. No one wants to hire a murder suspect, if that's what I am."

Isabella looked back at me sympathetically, which, while nice, wasn't as good as her solving the entire problem and clearing my name. Probably too much to ask.

As I ate my crab sandwich—the crab succulent, the mayonnaise creamy, the sourdough bread fresh and tangy—I gazed around the restaurant and almost choked. Looking back at me was Jason's biggest competitor and lifelong nemesis, Leon Haskell. I wasn't a fan myself, having had an uncomfortable meeting with him at his restaurant the year before.

"What's *he* doing here?" I said.

"Who?" Isabella took the opportunity to grab a handful of my french fries. She'd already eaten all of hers. Because of my great fondness for her, I didn't object.

"Leon Haskell," I said. "The owner of Scales and Fins."

Isabella gave a discreet look over to Leon's table. "That's weird. I've never waited on him before. I remember you telling me he lives in Seaside Shores."

"Yes. But he has his own restaurant. Why come here?"

She shrugged. "He wanted to try our food. Nothing wrong with that. Uh, oh. Don't look now but he's coming over."

Leon strolled over to our table. He was as slender as I remembered and still wore a beard.

"I believe we've met," he said, holding out his hand to me.

Reluctantly, I shook his clammy hand, inwardly cringing.

"It's Kayla Jeffries, correct?" he said. "You live here in Seaside Shores and run a baking business from your home."

"Yes, that's right." My eyes darted to Isabella.

"You misrepresented yourself a couple of months ago when you came into my restaurant. You said you were from out of town and visiting your aunt."

This, unfortunately, was true. I'd thought it possible he was Trudy's murderer and I'd been trying to get information out of him. I didn't respond.

Isabella said to fill the silence, "So?"

Leon ignored her. "You're a liar and a murder suspect," he said to me. "I want you to know I'm on to you. I saw the news about the hotel murder on TV. Your name and picture were front and center."

My picture? On TV?

"And," Leon said, pausing for maximum effect, "you are a thief."

"*What*?" I said, much too loudly. Everyone in the restaurant turned to stare at me. He may have been right about my suspect status and technically about the liar part, but I most certainly was not a thief.

"You stole a cloth napkin when you were at my restaurant," he said.

"She did not. She would never do that," Isabella said.

He had yet to acknowledge Isabella, and I could tell she was becoming more and more indignant. If there was one thing Isabella hated, it was being ignored.

"I advise you to never come into my restaurant again," Leon said imperiously.

"Like she'd want to?" Isabella said. "By the way, this is *my* restaurant." This was stretching the truth, but I nodded in assent. "And I'd like you to leave."

He at last turned his attention to Isabella. "No problem. I won't be back. The food is mediocre at best." He turned on his heel and walked back to his table. He threw a few bills onto his dirty plate and left the room.

We watched after him for a few beats without speaking.

"The nerve of that guy," Isabella said.

My stomach was in knots. "Iz, I can't believe my picture was on television. And they called me a suspect?"

"Yeah, it's getting to be a pretty big deal. Any ideas?"

"I'm going to continue my investigations and clear my name. *That's* my idea."

"Okay. Good."

"There's something else."

"What?"

"I think he's right. I did take the napkin."

AT HOME, I FOUND THE CARDIGAN SWEATER I'd worn the day in December when I went to Scales and Fins to talk to Leon. It was easy to remember because it was one of my least favorite garments— way too scratchy against my skin. I hadn't put it on since and wasn't sure why I hadn't thrown it into the ocean.

I took a deep breath and checked the right-hand pocket. I pulled out a cloth napkin. It was all true—I was a thief. I vaguely recalled stuffing the napkin into my pocket rather than placing it on the table at the end of my meal. I'd been undone by Leon's invitation to go to dinner with him and didn't really know what I was doing.

I ran the napkin through my fingers. It was rather lovely, blue and green with a fish pattern. I'd never stolen anything in my life. Now what? Should I launder it and mail it back to Leon? I would have to think about what to do next.

PUTTING THE ISSUE OF LEON HASKELL and the stolen napkin on the back burner, I sent friend requests to everyone who had commented on Edward's Facebook page below his mother's post. I immediately got an acceptance followed by a nasty private message. Stephanie Paymer, whose profile said she worked at Edward's restaurant, Spatula, had recognized my name from the news and had plenty to say. I gave up on that line of inquiry and spent way too long afterward sulking over what she had said. Wanting some perspective, I decided to call my mother.

I hadn't told Mom and my stepdad, Bob, about the murder yet. They'd been away at a "digital detox" spa for Valentine's Day and wouldn't have heard about it on the news. They were due to drive home that afternoon, so I dialed Mom's cell phone number.

Bob answered the phone and told me Mom was driving. After we'd exchanged greetings, he regaled me with a few movie facts he'd learned from a book he'd read during the detox. I tried to participate in the conversation but my heart wasn't in it.

"Is something wrong, sweetheart?" he asked.

"I have to tell you and Mom something. Can you put me on speaker?"

"Of course."

After a second, I heard Mom's voice. "Hi, darling. How are you?"

"I'm okay. Something happened that I want to talk to you both about. Tell me first how you enjoyed the spa."

"Oh, it was lovely," Mom said. "It was so nice not to be plugged in all the time. We read and rested and went for long walks. Sheer heaven."

"We're considering a 'no device' day at home every Sunday," Bob said.

I told them that sounded good.

"What did you want to talk to us about?" Mom asked. "Is it about the Valentine's event at The Countryside? How did it go? How did your desserts come out? Did you see your father?"

I launched into the story of the murder and the aftermath, including all the cancellations I'd sustained as a result, doing my best to be forthcoming as well as reassuring. There was a long silence when I finished.

"You guys there?" I asked.

"I hardly know what to say," Mom said. "That's beyond horrible."

"Are you all right?" Bob asked.

"Yes. I wasn't hurt. And I'm coming to terms with the emotional side of it."

"But you might be a suspect?" Mom asked. "How can that be?"

"I think it's only because I was in a class with the victim in college. Don't worry, though. Dad and I are going to clear my name. He's been a great help."

"Do you have any thoughts on who did it?" Bob said.

I gave them a brief summary of my theories.

"Those are all sound motives," Mom said. "Revenge, love, and money. Although I agree that Brenda doesn't seem likely because she won the TV competition over Edward."

I told her about the Facebook message and she advised me to do my best to put it out of my mind. "You know you didn't murder him, darling. And you're doing everything you can to find the real killer."

"You cracked the last case, Kayla," Bob said. "You can do it again."

"But be careful," Mom warned. "And call if you need us."

I promised I would be careful and we said good-bye. For a moment, I basked in the knowledge that I was getting along well with all three of my parents and that they got along with each other. How lucky was I?

VICKY CALLED LATER THAT EVENING ABOUT the family gathering she'd told me about when I saw her with Angie on the walking path. She asked if I'd help her brainstorm ideas for sandwiches and salads.

We settled on a spinach and artichoke appetizer inside a hollowed-out round loaf of sourdough bread, starfish-shaped sandwiches stuffed with crab, and a green salad.

"I think I can handle all of that," Vicky said.

I suggested I bake a lemon cake with sea-green frosting, decorated with white chocolate shells and starfish.

"That sounds perfect. John loves lemon."

"I'll do a test cake soon," I promised. "And make any tweaks necessary."

I was ready to hang up, but Vicky lingered on the line.

"Anything else?" I asked.

"Kayla, it's just . . . I saw your picture on the news."

I sighed. "I know. Do you want to cancel?"

"What? No, of course not. I wanted to say I'm sorry. I know you didn't murder anyone."

"Thanks. I'm afraid some of my other clients aren't as convinced of that."

"If there's anything I can do to help, let me know."

I thanked her and we hung up. Before jotting down what we'd discussed for the lemon cake, I turned over the idea of giving Det. Hernandez a list of personal references. I immediately dismissed the thought when I pictured him telling me the police dealt in facts, not opinions.

AN HOUR LATER, I HAD THE NEWS on low and was reading my cozy mystery on the couch. I screamed bloody murder when I looked up and saw a picture of myself halfway through the broadcast. My photo and name, along with Christie's and Hugo's, were arranged in an artistic circle around a full-length shot of Edward in chef's whites. Though we were termed "persons of interest" and not suspects, Christie, Hugo, and I looked guilty next to Edward's neatly-dressed and -coiffed form.

I'd never seen a worse photo of myself. My eyes were closed, my face was red and blotchy, and my hair was sticking out all over the place. Ah, ha! A security camera must have caught me as I entered the hotel lobby on the day of the murder. Double indignity. Not only on the news as a person of interest but an unflattering picture besides.

The circle of chefs disappeared, and a live shot of Leon Haskell filled up the screen. I stared at him for a few seconds before I raised the volume. He was calling me a liar, just as he'd said to me at the clubhouse restaurant. He went on to discuss my "charade" at his restaurant, calling it "incredibly suspicious" and indicative of a "shady character." He added that I'd walked off with something belonging to the restaurant. When the reporter asked what, he got cagey. He probably wanted it to sound worse than it already was.

As icing on the cake, he named my business and said I lived in Seaside Shores.

The phone rang. Jason.

"Are you watching the local news, by any chance?" he asked softly.

"Unfortunately, yes."

"You went to go see Leon at his restaurant?"

I gulped. I'd never told Jason I'd gone to see his nemesis. This was not going to get me back in his good graces.

"I was trying to find out if he killed Trudy. I thought maybe she was blackmailing him."

"You never told me." His tone was more disappointed than reproachful.

"I know," I said. "That was wrong of me. I apologize."

"I want to return to that sometime, but what's happening now is more important. I'm so sorry, Kayla."

"Thanks." I looked to the screen. Fortunately, Leon was gone, and the weatherman was holding forth. More windy days were expected over the next few weeks.

"Are you still going to San Francisco?" Jason asked.

I blew out a breath. "Yes."

"Okay. I want you to be careful and call me when you get back, all right?"

"I will. I promise."

We said good-bye, quite cordially. But I didn't want cordial. I wanted teasing and compliments and hugs and kisses—I wanted us back to how we used to be.

Meanwhile, I was sure to get even more cancellations now that I'd been branded a liar and a thief on television. I decided I'd have an early night. I went to bed to continue my book.

Sugar had just climbed onto my chest when an idea hit me. A security camera at the hotel had caught me entering the front door. What if there were cameras in the kitchen? If so, was it possible they were battery-powered and worked in the dark? Maybe the footage could ID the killer.

I got up to call Detective Hernandez. He answered after one ring. "Ah, Ms. Jeffries," he said. "It's been a while. I've missed you." Funny guy. I asked him about the cameras.

"No. No cameras in the kitchen. Did you really think we wouldn't have thought of that?'

I mumbled an apology of sorts and hung up, mad at myself. Of course the police would have checked on any available security footage. I was overtired and not thinking clearly. I put my book away, willing myself to fall asleep.

CHAPTER 8

T HE NEXT MORNING, THE CATS AND I went out to the patio again, early this time. The sun was rising, and pretty pink streaks lit up the sky, making me think of frosting. Again, Sugar caught a lizard and Flour did not. We went in after only ten minutes so I could get ready for the trip to San Francisco.

I took a long bath and dressed comfortably in jeans, a blue tee shirt, and a white sweater. After applying makeup and pulling my hair back into a ponytail, I gave the cats extra wet food and Meow Munchables—putting the diet on hold for yet another day—and locked up. I went outside to wait for Dad.

After a few seconds, my phone indicated an incoming email. I opened it and skimmed the content. Another cancellation, this time for a children's birthday party. Rats. I made a mental note to do as I had with my other emailed cancellations—write back to express my understanding and to ask that the client consider hiring me in the future.

Dad drove up as I put away my phone. He exited the car and came over. Hugging me gently, he asked, "Is this okay? I've been reading about HSPs. Sometimes they don't like being touched."

I was "touched" that he'd been researching. "That's true. But quick hugs are usually perfect."

"Okay. Good to know."

"Thanks for looking into it, Dad." We took our places in the car and drove off.

As we cruised onto the onramp to the freeway, I told Dad, "My name and picture were on the news last night. Even worse, a rival of Jason's was interviewed, and he called me a liar and a thief. He gave out my business name and said I live in Seaside Shores."

"You're joking."

"I wish I were." I told him about my visit to Leon's restaurant the previous December and how I'd accidentally absconded with the napkin.

"All of that is completely understandable," Dad said after I'd finished the story. "You were trying to solve your friend's murder. You were only doing what you felt you had to. And the napkin theft was an honest mistake."

"Thanks, but he never said what I stole, so it looks bad."

"We have to break this case," Dad said. "Pronto."

SHORTLY BEFORE NOON, WE ARRIVED IN SAN FRANCISCO to Balsamic, the restaurant where Hugo had said Christie returned looking for a job after the murder. Dad and I were both hungry so decided the best course of action was to order lunch and make our inquiries at the same time. I stepped out of the car. The day was overcast and a couple of raindrops hit the top of my head.

As we walked to the entrance, a pleasant smell of meat cooking streamed from the restaurant. My stomach growled in response.

The host told us there would be a ten-minute wait and directed us to a couple of seats in the lobby area. I looked around but didn't see Christie. After fifteen minutes, the host escorted us to a table near the kitchen. When we asked if Christie was there, he said he didn't know.

We placed our napkins on our laps and opened the menus.

"I think I'll have the asparagus soup and green salad," I said to Dad.

"That's all? I'm treating, you know. Especially now that you're experiencing business troubles. Please have whatever you want."

"Thanks. That's really nice." I changed my mind to a steak sandwich with fries. Dad said that sounded good and he'd order the same thing. We agreed to have cheesecake for dessert if we weren't too full.

When the waiter came over, we asked about Christie. He said she hadn't worked there for three years.

"But she came back here looking for a job, right?" I asked.

"I wouldn't know. I've been on vacation."

"Would you be able to talk to us about her?" Dad said.

"And do you know anything about her relationship with Edward Winthrop?" I followed up.

His eyes flicked over us. "I didn't know her that well. And I don't have any clue about her relationships."

"Is there anyone else we can talk to? The manager?" I asked.

"She's not here today."

I persisted, "Could we talk to the other waitstaff?"

"No. Everyone's busy."

He left to help the patron at the next table without taking our orders. Dad and I looked at each other.

"The prices *are* quite expensive," he said.

"Bail?"

He nodded. We replaced our napkins on the table and left.

"You know, she was pretty passionate about him," a voice said as we walked to the car. "Both positive and negative. He's the guy who was just murdered, right?"

We wheeled around to see a woman coming out of Balsamic. I remembered her as one of the waitstaff. She had her car keys in one hand and was obviously on her way out.

"Do you mean Christie and Edward?" I asked. "Did you hear us?"

She removed her nametag—which read Heidi—and said, "Yes and yes. Christie and Edward had one of those dysfunctional relationships. They broke up, got back together, broke up again . . . you get the picture. One minute they'd be all over each other and the next they'd be hurting each other any way they could. She took it to the limit one time when she was working here."

"What did she do?" I asked.

"Threatened him with poultry scissors. He was up here visiting her and came to the restaurant one day. He said something to her that made her go berserk."

Wondering if this was the smoking gun, I asked breathlessly, "What did he say?"

"I missed that part. Sorry."

"Do you have any idea where she is?" Dad said.

"She *was* here, like you thought, looking for a job, but we don't have any openings. She said she was going to drive over to Springvale. She'd heard there was an opening at Lombardi's."

We thanked her and continued on to the car.

"Springvale, huh?" Dad said. He turned on the ignition.

"Coincidental, isn't it?"

Mom and Dad had raised me in Springvale, and my mother still lived there. We were all familiar with Lombardi's, having eaten there many times. Mom had such a fondness for the Italian eatery that she'd held her wedding to Bob there. The restaurant dished up huge servings of spaghetti and meatballs and pasta with pesto following the ceremony in the garden. The dessert chef made a big batch of tiramisu which acted as the wedding cake and I'd never gotten over how delicious it was. I'd experimented once or twice with making my own version of the coffee dessert, but I'd never been able to pull off what Lombardi's could do.

"We can swing by Lombardi's to have lunch and look for Christie," Dad said.

"That sounds great." We headed for the onramp to the freeway.

Once we were on the highway, my phone rang. I checked the caller ID and said, "It's Detective Hernandez."

"You better answer."

I took the call. "Hello?"

Forgoing a greeting, Det. Hernandez said, "Ms. Jeffries, we'd like you to come into the station again at your earliest convenience."

"Um. Okay," I said. "It won't be for a while. I'm out of town at the moment."

"Please come in when you get back. We'll see you soon."

I got off the phone. "I wonder what's up now." I twirled my ring around on my finger. "This can't be good."

"It'll be okay, K-Bear. Just go in and tell the truth."

He'd said the same thing before my first interview and it hadn't helped much.

"Do you think we should hire a lawyer?" I asked.

"It's something to think about. Let's see how this meeting goes. My friend in Napa might have recommendations. He's a lawyer himself."

"Okay. I can't believe he wants me to come back. What could it be about?"

"I don't know, honey. But let's talk about something else so you don't have to think about it right now. Tell me more about the HSP trait." We pulled onto the lower deck of the Bay Bridge. "I want to understand it—and you—better."

"If you tell me the truth," I said. "Did you ever read the information I sent you?"

Dad didn't answer. He looked like he was trying to formulate a response but couldn't come up with one.

"It's okay. Really," I said. "I know that at first blush, HSPs look . . . I don't know. Weak, I guess. Overly dramatic about things. Believe me, I often have moments when I think that."

"No. I would never say that," Dad said. "But I'm sure I have misunderstandings about what it's like. Tell me how it was for you when you were a child. I remember a few things. We went to see an Impressionist exhibit at the de Young, the three of us. You were in heaven. I didn't know that children could have such strong reactions to art. But that's part of it, right?"

"It is. Art and nature are very important to HSPs. I think I remember that exhibit. I love Impressionists. My landlord, Tristan, gave me a painting that reminds me of Monet's work. It's over the fireplace. You can see it when you come over."

"That's wonderful," Dad said.

I thought for a moment. "I remember our Girl Scout troop going to a candle store around Christmastime. I loved the smells. But I remember bad smells too. Mom used to make liver and onions and I hated it."

"Well, I'm with you there. I don't know why she made that. She didn't like it, I didn't like it, and you didn't like it. I think liver is supposed to be good for you, though."

"I think I'd rather be unhealthy."

Dad laughed. "What else?"

"My biggest triggers for overstimulation are touch and noise. I can't stand a lot of sounds. Lawn mowers, leaf blowers, dogs barking, that kind of thing. I know most people don't like those noises but HSPs have a more difficult time blocking them out."

Dad nodded. "And being touched bothers you at times."

"Yes. Sometimes it's okay and other times I don't like it, usually if I'm already overstimulated. But it's not just people. I dislike scratchy fabrics against my skin. On the other hand, I love curling up under a blanket. Jason gave me a weighted one for Christmas and it's great for stress."

"Good. I'll try to remember all of that."

"Thanks, Dad."

"I like getting to know you. Again."

I smiled at him. "Likewise. This has been terrific."

At Lombardi's, we asked the hostess if Christie was now on staff. She said she didn't think so, but she'd go check. She came back to say that Christie had been there looking for a job, but they'd already filled the open chef position. We'd struck out once again.

"You don't have any contact information for Christie?" Dad asked me when the hostess stepped away.

"No. I could call Conrad and probably get her cell phone number, but I prefer to talk to people in person. They tend to be more forthcoming face-to-face."

"You sound like a pro."

"I don't want to be a professional at this. Baking, yes. Detective work, no."

"I hear you. We might as well eat. I've passed hungry and moved on to starving."

"Me too."

As we waited for a table, Dad picked up a discarded newspaper. He handed me the puzzles at my request, and he turned to the news. After a minute, I looked up to see him folding up part of the paper and placing it at the end of the bench.

"Dad?"

"It's nothing."

"Let me guess. The murder? Me? Me in association with the murder?"

"Nothing you haven't seen already."

"It's all right," I said. "You don't have to protect me."

"Soon this will all be over," Dad said so convincingly that I almost believed him.

We were taken to our table a few minutes later. Dad and I agreed to order a deep-dish olive and mushroom pizza, which, when it arrived, hit the spot for us both.

"I remember this pizza," Dad said. "We had it after your college graduation."

"You're right. Graduation was the first time you met Bob. I was so nervous about the two of you meeting each other."

"I didn't know that, sweetheart. He and I got along fine. We were all so proud of you."

I brushed away a tear. "That means a lot to me."

After we'd each had four slices of pizza and scooped up and eaten the olives and mushrooms that had fallen off onto the platter, we shared a piece of the beloved tiramisu. Dad paid the bill, I left the tip, and we returned to the car.

Dad said as we approached Los Robles on our way back to Oceanville, "Since we're nearby, how about going to see Detective Hernandez?"

The idea filled me with dread, but it made sense to get it over with. "Okay."

He took the exit for the police station. Once more we parked on the street and went inside.

At the desk, I identified myself and said Det. Hernandez had wanted me to come in. The officer told me she'd let him know I was there.

Dad handed me a sand dollar.

"What's this?" I whispered.

"I found it on the beach yesterday. For luck." He winked at me.

Detective Hernandez appeared, we went through the security door, and he led me down the hallway to an interview room. This was new. We'd always met in his office before. I hoped it didn't mean anything.

When we were seated, I rubbed the sand dollar in my palm.

With no niceties this time, the detective said, "We have information that you were romantically involved with Edward Winthrop. First you told us you didn't know him. Then you said the two of you had been in a class together but hardly spoke to each other. Now we've found out you and he were in a relationship. I'd like an explanation."

I stared back at him for a few seconds, emotions bubbling up inside of me. A relationship? Romantically involved? How could he say such a thing?

Keeping my voice as even as possible, I said, "Like I told you, I did realize after the murder that we'd gone to college at the same time. He was going by Ted then. We had one class together, only one, in which we barely interacted with each other. We didn't have a relationship of any kind, not even a friendship. That's the absolute truth. I don't know where you're getting your information, but it's not correct."

We did our mutual staring thing. Then the detective made a couple of notes on his pad and said, "All right. You can go for now. We'll be in touch."

I let out a long breath and went to collect Dad. I silently handed him the sand dollar and he put it back in his pocket.

I told him about the interview as soon as we were out of earshot of anyone in the station.

Dad's jaw fell when I relayed what Det. Hernandez had said. "How is that possible?" he asked.

"I have no idea. I'm gonna find out, though, I can tell you that."

THAT EVENING, WHEN DAD WAS BACK at his hotel and I was alone again, I cuddled up with the cats and watched the news, hoping I'd gain some insight into Det. Hernandez's statement. An assistant professor of English at UC Springvale, Elliott Twining, was interviewed ten minutes into the broadcast. I recognized the university's clock tower behind him.

"I was good friends with Edward Winthrop in college," Twining told the eager reporter. "He went by Ted back then. He and Kayla Jeffries were joined at the hip. Except when they were fighting, that is. When he broke it off with her for good, she was mad. I'm not saying she killed him, but if they met up all these years later, maybe the old feelings resurfaced."

It was one thing to hear the falsehood from Detective Hernandez and another to see it on TV. "That is a load of bullpucky, as Hugo says," I objected out loud, my tone scaring the cats. They jumped down from the couch.

The reporter now spoke directly to the camera. "Detective David Hernandez of the Los Robles police says they are looking into the possibility." The story turned to a burglary at a restaurant in La Tierra.

My cheeks felt hot. I went into the kitchen and splashed cold water on my face. I had to calm down and think this through. Now I knew where Det. Hernandez had gotten the false information, but it didn't explain why Twining said what he did. Was he confusing me with someone else?

I decided I would go see him and find out. I called Dad and told him my plan. He offered to go with me and we set a time for the next day.

"We'll set things straight with this guy and make sure Detective Hernandez gets the correct information," Dad said before we hung up. I agreed, once again happy that my father was by my side.

CHAPTER 9

THE NEXT MORNING, I SIPPED MY USUAL DECAF COFFEE and made scrambled eggs with toast. I had a quick shower, dressed in jeans and a silky blouse, and tied my hair back in a braid. After applying lipstick and mascara, I checked my phone and was stunned to find I had several voice mails and emails from reporters. What the heck? The messages all asked about my "college relationship" with Edward. I deleted them all.

When I left the house ten minutes later, a woman came up to me on the driveway. She thrust her phone in my face.

"Kayla Jeffries? Toni LaValle from The Ocean County Tribune."

"Please go away. You're on private property."

"You had a relationship with Edward Winthrop in college. What was he like back then? How did the two of you get along? Who broke up with whom? What happened when you saw him again at The Countryside Inn?"

Remembering what Dad and I had practiced, I said as calmly as I could, "I'm very sorry about Edward Winthrop's death. But I had nothing to do with it. Yes, I was in a college class with him, but we had no interaction, let alone a relationship. I hope his killer is caught soon. Thank you."

Before Toni could ask more questions, I walked around her, unlocked the mini-van, got in, and sped off.

Heart thumping from the encounter, I checked the gas gauge. Nearly empty. I swung into a station just outside Seaside Shores. As I topped off the tank, I looked up at the sky, trying to calm my nerves. It was perfectly clear and would be a nice day to get some exercise on the coastal path. Hopefully, I could get in a walk soon; it would be good for my stress level, which was rising rapidly.

I picked up Dad at his hotel and told him about the messages from the reporters and the in-person visit from Toni LaValle.

"It sounds like you handled everything exactly right."

"Thanks. I'm glad we talked over what I would say. I was ready."

We drove straight-through, arriving at UC Springvale in under three hours. Finding a parking lot, I slid into a space. Dad and I went to the machine and paid for sixty minutes.

A wave of nostalgia hit me as we made it onto the campus. I hadn't been especially social in college, no surprise there, but I'd enjoyed my classes. At the time, I rented a small studio on the second floor of a building within walking distance of the university. As tiny as the apartment was, I'd adored my first grown-up home. I spent as much time there as possible, reading and falling in love with the books assigned for my literature classes.

Dad and I headed to Taylor Hall, where I remembered the English department was located. We found out from the office receptionist that Twining was currently finishing up a seminar on the Brontës in Lecture Hall B.

Dad and I sneaked into the lecture hall and took seats in the back. Twining was a charismatic teacher, and the subject matter appealed to me. I remembered taking a class on the Brontës fifteen years earlier. I had fallen hard for the relationships between Cathy and Heathcliff and Jane and Rochester. I'd thought of them as so romantic. When I read the books again many years later, I wasn't so sure.

The class ended and we walked down to the front of the room to the lectern where a student and Twining were talking. A line had formed behind the enthusiastic young woman, who was gesturing with both arms. I hadn't remembered Twining from college and seeing him in person did nothing to refresh my memory.

When it was our turn to talk to him, Dad gestured to me but I became tongue-tied.

Twining regarded me curiously as though he couldn't quite place me. He looked at Dad, similarly puzzled. He said at last, "Two of our older students. Fantastic."

That loosened my tongue. "I'm Kayla Jeffries. This is my father, Andrew. I'm here because you've been talking about me in connection with Edward Winthrop's murder."

"Ah, yes," he said. Before he could go on, the three of us became aware of a couple of students in the line watching us with obvious interest. One took out his phone, presumably to film this mini-drama. Twining glanced over at them.

"I'll be in my office, B-30, in five minutes," he said. "Meet me there?"

I decided I, too, would prefer the meeting to be private. I nodded. Twining turned his attention to the next student in line and Dad and I left the lecture hall.

We located B-30 and waited outside the door. Twining arrived five minutes later. He invited us in and motioned to two chairs, each with a tower of books on the seats. His desk was a mess and couldn't hold another thing. We stacked the books on the floor.

Twining took off his blazer and folded it over his chair back. He sat down and took a swig of water from a bottle on his desk.

"I only told the truth," he said, directing his statement at me. "When I saw your name and picture on the news, it clicked. I knew Ted pretty well and I remembered his girlfriend. I checked my yearbook, and there you were in lots of pictures with him. I contacted the detective in charge of the case—Hernandez, I think his name is."

I looked back at him in disbelief. One of us was incredibly mistaken. Sure, college was a long time ago, but I would know if I'd been in an intense relationship.

"That's impossible," I said.

Twining swung his chair around to pull a yearbook from his stuffed bookshelf. He opened the book to a sticky note and pointed to a photo.

Dad and I leaned forward for a better look. Though of course he looked younger than he had at the hotel, Edward was easily recognizable. The chiseled features and haughty expression were the same.

I examined the petite girl gazing up at Edward with adoring eyes.

"Elliott, this is *not* me," I said. "The girl's name isn't even given. The caption just says, 'Sigma Alpha Epsilon President Ted Winthrop and girlfriend.'"

He showed us three more pictures of Edward and the girl, all with the same captioning, then found and pointed to a portrait in the seniors section. It was the same girl, the same girl who wasn't me. But "Kayla Elizabeth Jeffries" was the name underneath the picture, which was *my* name. What the heck? How had I never noticed this? I looked over the rest of the page and saw a photo of myself with the name "Kaycee Ellen Jeffs" underneath. I showed it to Edward.

"*This* is me," I said. "They reversed the pictures. This was his girlfriend, Kaycee Jeffs. Yes, our names are similar and we look alike, but she has blue eyes and I have brown. And her lips are fuller and our noses are different shapes."

Twining peered at me closely and then looked down at the yearbook. "Good grief. What a terrible mistake. What can I do to fix it?"

"The most important thing is to call Detective Hernandez," I said. "Can you call him? Now?"

"Yes. I believe I have his number right here." Twining rooted through the papers on his desk and came up with a phone number. He picked up his office landline.

Twining left the detective a message saying he'd mistaken me for someone else and gave him the student's correct name. He apologized for the inconvenience and hung up.

"We'd like you to tell the reporter you talked to as well," Dad said. I beamed at him, so glad he was with me.

Twining looked up the number for the reporter and again left a message.

"Thank you," I said as Dad and I stood to leave.

"Do you have a business card?" Dad asked. "In case anything else comes up?"

Twining handed one to him. "Let me know if I can do anything else. I sincerely apologize."

We left his office and returned to the car. Our trip had been so short that our meter still had money on it.

"What do you think, honey?" Dad asked when we were on our way.

"I'm glad we cleared that up. I'm going to check in with Detective Hernandez when I get home, though, to be sure he got the message."

"I think that's smart. Hey, how about swinging by to see your mom and Bob before heading back to Oceanville?"

"Great idea."

As we drove into the Springvale hills to see my mother and stepfather, Dad said, "This is a nice area. I've never been over here, but I remember when they were building it."

After I was born in the 1980s, Mom and Dad and I moved into a house close to UC Springvale. The building was originally used for student housing, and my parents continued the tradition by renting out the basement to juniors and seniors. The students proved a source of endless fascination to me as they came and went, though I was too shy to talk to them.

The townhomes where Mom and Bob now lived were a relatively new addition to Springvale, having been built in the late 1990s.

"It *is* nice over here," I agreed. "There are nature trails and a stable too."

"Yes. Your mother said she often walks on the trails."

"I keep forgetting you talk on the phone with her," I said. "Speaking of which, do you think we should call and warn them?"

Dad got a mischievous look on his face. "I'd kind of like to surprise your mom."

"Okay, but you get to take the heat if it's not a pleasant surprise," I said. "They usually like people to call first."

Mom opened the door carrying a dish towel, and the towel and her jaw dropped at the same time. "Kayla! Andrew. My goodness."

"Hey, Mom. We were in the area—"

"And thought we'd stop by," Dad finished.

"Come in, come in. Bob's out meeting a friend. He'll be sad he missed you. May I get you some tea? Unless you'd like lunch? It's no problem to put something together. There's leftover casserole from last night and I could make a salad."

"I can't speak for Kayla, but that would be very nice, Diana," Dad said.

"It's okay, you can speak for me. I'm starving," I said, and we all laughed.

Dad looked into the living room and through the glass doors to the small garden in the back of the property. "You have a beautiful home here."

Mom smiled. "Thank you. That's nice of you to say."

He turned his attention back to her. "And you look just as beautiful."

She did look great. Her eyes were bright and her short brown hair had a few subtle blond highlights, perhaps from being out in the sun at the detox spa.

"Sit, sit," she said, directing us to the kitchen table. "Lunch will be ready in a jiff."

"Where's Callie?" I asked.

"Oh, you know her," Mom said. "She's napping on our bed, as usual."

"I won't bother her, then." Callie was a healthy 18-year-old calico cat, but she liked to sleep a lot.

Mom served up lunch a few minutes later. We covered a wide range of subjects as we ate: the October hurricane that barely bypassed Dad's city in Florida, the Spanish class Mom was taking at

the community college, and a few of my recent baking successes—
and failures. I didn't bring up the mishaps with Vincent, feeling
like a lawyer or therapist and wanting to maintain confidentiality.

The discussion inevitably turned to Edward's murder. We
rehashed everything we'd learned and didn't come up with
anything new, but Dad listened closely whenever Mom spoke and
they smiled at each other a lot.

Mom made tea and brought a plate of shortbread cookies to the
table. I'd learned everything I knew about baking from her, so of
course the treats were delicious. She boxed up a few for Dad and
me to take back to Oceanville.

"These are wonderful," Dad said, taking a bite of cookie. "I
think I remember them." Mom beamed at him.

They were sure getting along well. My parents were good as
friends, not so good as spouses. As much as the divorce had a
negative impact on me, it really had been the right decision for
them both—and eventually for me as well. My mother had found
happiness with Bob, and perhaps my father had found a potential
new mate with Stacy. I hoped so. He deserved to be happy.

Dad and I headed for the door about an hour later. He kissed
Mom on the cheek and she took his hand and held it for a few
beats. It was nice to see. I remembered the fights they'd had when
I was growing up. Fortunately, their arguments had never turned
physical, but there had been some yelling. Today was a memory of
the two I wouldn't mind keeping.

AFTER I LEFT DAD OFF AT HIS HOTEl, I went home, feeling tired. As
I drove down the driveway, I caught sight of a news van. I backed
up, turned onto Sea Lion Drive, and rounded the corner to Ocean
Lane to park. I went through my back gate, crossed the patio, and
entered my cottage through the sliding glass door.

Once I was settled, I peeked out the front window. The
news van was gone. Sighing in relief, I went into my bedroom
and rummaged around in my closet for my yearbooks. The cats
wandered in to "help," which of course hindered me instead. I

almost dropped a shoebox onto Flour when I reached up to the shelf above my clothes.

I finally located the yearbook that matched the one in Twining's office. I took it over to my bed and found the portrait section. My picture and name were correct. The yearbook editors must have realized the mix-up and fixed it, or perhaps Kaycee had caught the error and told them. In any case, Twining had the problem version.

I dug my phone from my pocket and took photos of the page as well as the ones with Kaycee and Edward. I'd send them to Det. Hernandez if he requested proof.

I dialed his number.

"Ms. Jeffries, hello. Any new information for us? Anything you'd like to confess?"

"No," I said, doing my best to remain on an even keel. "I didn't do anything so I have nothing to confess to. I want to know if you got the message from Elliott Twining, recanting what he told you about me."

"I did, yes."

"Okay. Good. He mistook me for someone else. I can send you proof if you like."

"Thank you, but that won't be necessary."

A thought occurred to me. "Have you heard anything from a man named Leon Haskell?"

"We have. His accusations have been dismissed as not being relevant."

Two pieces of good news. "Great. I'm done then, right? I'm not a person of interest or a suspect? Will you be issuing a statement saying I'm innocent?"

The detective let a beat go by before saying, "You were still in the kitchen at the time of the murder. And you had access to the weapon."

"But that's true of everyone else too. The difference is I don't have a motive. Like I keep saying, I had one class with Edward and scarcely spoke to him."

"Just because you weren't in a relationship with him doesn't mean you didn't have feelings for him. Maybe you killed him because he rejected you in college. Unrequited love is a powerful motive."

I rolled my eyes at Flour, who was twirling around on her back on the floor, and said to Det. Hernandez, "College was a long time ago. Edward didn't reject me, anyway. Plus, I didn't even remember him until after the murder."

"Call if you have any other news," he said and hung up.

I stared at my phone. What a vexing conversation. What more could I do to convince him of my innocence?

Hoping answers might come to me while I was cooking, I mixed up dough for four hand pies and refrigerated it for an hour. I made two veggie pies for dinner and ate them on the couch while watching TV. Back in the kitchen, I whipped up raspberry pies for dessert, using a cookie cutter to carve out shells on the top crusts. I loved how they turned out and decided I'd make them for Jason when things were better between us. I'd get his take on whether I should add the dessert pies to my business selections.

Although I hadn't come up with any new ways to convince Det. Hernandez of my innocence, I declared my evening successful. I spent the rest of the night reading my book.

AFTER MIDNIGHT, A THOUGHT WORMED ITS WAY through my consciousness and made me jolt upright in bed, my heart pounding. I had promised Jason I'd call him when I returned from the San Francisco trip with my dad the day before and I had forgotten. I knew he kept his phone volume up all night but I couldn't call him now, at this late hour. Because of the restaurant, he was an early riser, and I didn't want to disturb his sleep. I would make contact with him in the morning and let him know what I'd been up to.

EARLY THE NEXT MORNING, I CALLED JASON. He didn't answer. I left a message, apologizing for not phoning when I said I would, and bringing him up-to-date on my recent activities, downplaying anything related to Edward's murder. I then turned to the information in my logic grid.

For Hugo, I'd written "firing?" as his motive. Yes, he could have been mad that Edward let him go from his job. Not only did Edward take away Hugo's source of income but it would have been a black mark on the young chef's resume. The motive was solid, but Hugo seemed too naïve to be the killer, as I'd noted in my "Reasons Against" column. He didn't strike me as someone who could brutally stab another human being in the neck. He was a self-proclaimed klutz, said things like "bullpucky" and "dude," and enjoyed swinging on porch swings. I wasn't ready to remove him from the grid, but I had my doubts he'd committed the murder.

I looked next to what I had for Brenda. As motive, I'd written "*Premier Chef*" with a question mark after. But I couldn't figure out why she would kill Edward given *she* won the competition. Again, I didn't remove her in case I was missing something, like what I'd mentioned to Dad—perhaps Edward had something on her that nullified her win.

As for Christie, I'd written "relationship?" for the motive, but I didn't know where she was and hadn't been able to talk to her, so I had yet to form any kind of opinion on the likelihood of her being the killer. Feeling cranky, I put the grid away and turned my focus to my business.

I spent the rest of the morning making several batches of cupcakes for an office party. I added white chocolate otters to the top of each dessert, grateful that the client—a law firm downtown—hadn't cancelled.

When I delivered the cupcakes a few minutes after noon, I overheard two women talking about me.

"She's the one, isn't she?" one said.

"Yeah. Are we sure we want to eat these desserts?" the other responded.

I felt my face flush. They weren't even bothering to keep their voices down.

Trying to ignore the pain in the pit of my stomach, I announced to the room, "Hi, everyone. Cupcakes here! One is a vanilla cake with lemon filling and the other is chocolate with raspberry inside. Both have vanilla frosting."

The office manager, Jasmine, came forward, thanked me, and gave me a check. "Don't worry about those two," she whispered to me, nodding her head to the women. "They just like gossip."

I smiled. It was good to know that not *everyone* thought I was a killer.

AFTER THE OFFICE PARTY, I HAD SOME FREE TIME in my schedule, so I stopped by the history museum a few streets over from the law firm. Hearing that Seaside Shores had been built on the site of an old amusement park had made me curious.

Admission to the museum was free, but donations were encouraged. In the lobby, I pushed a few dollars into the donation box, greeted the volunteer at the desk, and stepped inside the main room.

I soon found what I was looking for. An entire wing of the museum was devoted to Playworld. I delighted in the old photos on display, smiling at the serious looks of the patrons when posing and the clothing that completely covered up their bodies. In all the pictures, the beach portion of the amusement park was packed with visitors, attesting to the attraction's popularity.

A map of Playworld and a tabletop model drew my attention next. In addition to the merry-go-round of Tristan's painting, the park had featured a roller coaster, Ferris wheel, and a fun house including a long slide. An expansive outdoor pool right on the beach had also been a big selling point.

I was particularly interested to read that cottages had been constructed in the late 1920s for overnight stays. I wished those had survived. I could have been living in one a century later, assuming, of course, it had been updated for the times.

Before going home, I stopped by the gift shop and picked up something for Jason, in hopes we might someday exchange late Valentine's gifts.

That evening, I caught Elliott Twining on the news, retracting what he'd said about my relationship with Edward. The same reporter who'd interviewed him the first time pressed him, asking if he was positive Edward and I hadn't been involved. Twining explained about the blunder with the yearbook pictures. He came off well, and I ticked that worry off my list. I hoped the reporters would leave me alone once and for all.

Checking in with Vicky after the news, I was happy to learn that her husband's birthday party was still a go and she wanted me to provide the dessert.

"Great," I said. "I've been giving lessons to Vincent at the clubhouse restaurant. I'll do a test cake with him tomorrow."

The next morning, I supervised Vincent as he made the vanilla cake layers. He was careful with the ingredients and the rounds looked perfect when I placed them in the oven. I had a good feeling that we were headed for a breakthrough.

While the layers baked, I oversaw him as he made the vanilla frosting. When it was done, I showed him how to color it with sea-green food gel.

"That's really pretty," I said. "Good work. Can you check on the cakes?"

He put down the spoon he'd been using to mix in the gel, picked up a dish towel, and went to the oven. He opened the door and used the cloth to remove one of the layers. I realized too late that he'd used the towel he'd burned a hole through during our pie lesson. He was now touching the pan with his bare hands.

"Aaah! Hot!" he cried, dropping the cloth and releasing the pan from his hands onto the stove. It dangled precariously from the edge. In my haste to grab a potholder, I knocked the bowl of frosting off the counter. The bowl didn't break but the frosting went everywhere. I slipped and fell to the floor. The cake pan—the hot cake pan—plopped into my lap. I shoved it off me, whimpering in pain.

I looked up at Vincent and he looked down at me. We burst into laughter.

"You should see your face," he said.

"You should see yours!"

"Seriously, are you okay?" he asked.

"I think so. You?"

"Mostly."

We tended to our burns, cleaned up, and began again. While I took care of the cake layers, Vincent worked on his own to mix the gel into the frosting. It came out a sickly green color. Moving on from that failure, I had him make the seashells for the top of the cake. They ended up as unrecognizable blobs.

"Good work, Vincent," I said insincerely as we sampled our finished product.

"You don't have to say that," he said. "But it tastes good."

"It does," I agreed. "I better get going." I left, secretly glad I'd be working alone on the actual cake for Vicky's party.

JASON AND I EXCHANGED A FEW TEXTS over the remainder of the weekend. I told him about Elliott Twining's retraction and once more apologized for failing to contact him when I got back from San Francisco. He responded by saying he understood. That was encouraging.

On Monday, I got out my grid and looked it over, realizing I'd never talked with Detective Hernandez about Hugo. Although I didn't consider the young chef my most likely suspect, he did have a reasonable motive because Edward had fired him.

I'd been parking on Ocean Lane to avoid any unwelcome visits from the media, so I went out back to get my mini-van. I drove to Los Robles and asked once more to speak with Detective Hernandez.

"Ah, Ms. Jeffries. Here again, I see," the detective said when I came into his office. "Alone today? Something you'd like to tell me that you don't want your father to know about?"

"No. I just wanted to be sure you knew that Hugo worked for Edward a couple of years ago and Edward fired him."

He looked back at me impassively.

"Let me guess," I said. "Not new information?"

He leaned back in his chair. "Your words, not mine. Thanks for stopping by, Ms. Jeffries."

I blew out a long breath and left.

My stomach growled as I settled into the mini-van. I had a craving for something fatty and salty. I wouldn't mind sugary and creamy too. With all the choices of restaurants in Oceanville, I rarely ate fast food. But it was now past noon and I was ravenous. I couldn't be hungry for too long or I became irritable and not fit for human contact.

I swung into the first Los Robles drive-through I saw. The smell of grilled burgers emanating from the restaurant was intoxicating, so I rolled up to the first window and ordered a value deal of a cheeseburger, fries, and strawberry milkshake. I paid and drove forward.

I couldn't believe it when the elusive Christie Nelson handed over my bag of food at the second window. She recognized me at the same time.

"Oh, you. Great," she said.

"Christie. What are you doing here?"

She bristled. "It's all I could find for the time being. I needed a job."

"Of course. No judgment. I'm sorry it didn't work out at the hotel." I didn't add Balsamic and Lombardi's to the list of jobs that didn't come to fruition.

"Here's your shake," she said, passing it to me. "Could you please go?" She turned away.

"Wait, Christie," I said. "Can I just ask you something?"

"There are cars behind you. This is a busy time of day."

"It'll only take a second."

"Okay. But hurry up."

"It's about your relationship with Edward," I said, looking at her closely for her reaction.

"What relationship with Edward?"

"I know you were involved with him."

She held my gaze without answering.

"Come on, Christie. I'm trying to figure out who killed him. Don't you want your name cleared? You can't like being a person of interest or possible suspect, or whatever we are. The police know you and Edward had a romance at one time. There's no need to keep it a secret."

"I have a break in fifteen minutes. I'll meet you in your car. Go park over there." She pointed to a corner of the lot.

I did as she said and ate my lunch as I waited for her. It hit the spot and was better than I wanted it to be. A few cherry trees in the parking lot were blooming and I enjoyed looking at them as I sipped on my shake.

Exactly fifteen minutes later, Christie opened the passenger door of the mini-van and climbed in. I wiped my mouth and turned to her.

She sighed heavily. "Okay, look. It's true that Edward and I were in a relationship. I thought we were going to get married. Two chefs. Cute, right? But it all started to go south when we were in a small competition together. I beat him, and he couldn't stand it. He accused me of cheating. Honestly, I think he believed deep down that women can't be chefs. Sure, they can follow a recipe and end up with a meal, but nothing restaurant-quality. We went through cycles of breaking up and getting back together after that. When he won runner-up on *Premier Chef,* that was the death knell of the relationship." She grimaced, as if realizing "death" wasn't the best word choice. "I didn't kill him."

"But you had a history."

She turned away from me and looked out the window. "Yes, but I was over him by the time I saw him at the hotel. He meant nothing to me."

"I heard the two of you had a fight at Balsamic. You threatened him with poultry scissors, which aren't that far off from cooking shears."

She turned back. "Not that rumor again. I happened to be holding the poultry scissors while we were arguing. I wasn't going to *stab* him. And I didn't stab him with the shears at the hotel. I swear." She spoke with sincerity in her voice. I believed her.

"Do you have any ideas who *did* kill him?"

"Honestly, I have no clue. I assumed he'd annoyed you or Hugo so much that you'd had it. I know he could be abrasive at times and he was being a jerk during dinner prep."

"Yeah, he was. But I didn't do it. Hugo might have, though I'm having my doubts. Do you think it's possible Brenda could be the killer?"

She thought that over for a minute. "She was definitely there when it happened, wasn't she? And they were on *Premier Chef* together."

"Right. But she won and Edward didn't. Did he ever say anything about that to you? Was he suspicious that she'd won, thinking she didn't deserve to, or anything like that?"

Christie shook her head. "No. He just thought he was god's gift because he got runner-up."

"Okay."

"I have to get moving," she said. "I want to grab something other than burger and fries before I go back." She hesitated, then reached into my empty food bag. She dug a pen from her purse and scribbled a phone number on my receipt.

"If you want to talk again, feel free to contact me," she said. "You're right, I don't like being involved in this. If you can work this thing out, I'd be grateful."

I reciprocated by giving her one of my business cards and telling her she could call or email me anytime. I took off for home, mulling over our meeting. I'd found her denial credible, but *someone* wasn't telling the truth. The only thing I knew for certain was that *I* didn't murder Edward. I had forgotten how frustrating detective work could be.

TURNING TO MY BUSINESS, I made the birthday cake for Vicky's husband, John, the next day. It came out considerably better than it had with Vincent. I loaded the dessert into the mini-van a little before five.

John and his guests were playing croquet on the front lawn of the family's home on Wave Street. An elderly woman, who might have been John's grandmother, smacked a yellow ball with her mallet, sending it crashing into a blue one. Everyone clapped.

Angie saw me and skipped over. Once more, she wore her heart-shaped sunglasses and looked undeniably cool.

"Hi, Kayla! Can I see the cake?"

I'd made Angie's birthday cake the year before and she'd been my biggest fan ever since. "Sure. Is your mom in the kitchen?"

She nodded. I waved to the croquet players and we went inside.

Vicky was busy preparing the crab sandwiches, which looked so good I started salivating.

I flipped up the top of the bakery box to show Vicky and Angie my lemon cake with sea-green frosting. I was rather proud of the white chocolate shells and starfish I'd made from molds, thinking they looked very elegant on top of the cake.

"Wow," Angie said, her mouth dropping open.

"Wow squared," Vicky agreed. "John will love it." She handed me the check she'd already written out. "Kayla, you're welcome to stay for the party. We have plenty of food."

"Thanks. That's really nice of you. But I think I'll head home. Hope you have a good time."

I went home and had a classic introvert evening, reading and cuddling up with the cats. But I didn't have as good a time as I might have. The reason was simple; I wished Jason was reading on the other side of the couch.

CHAPTER 10

JASON CALLED THE NEXT MORNING AND I was so surprised to hear from him that I couldn't even say hello. Although we'd been exchanging texts, we hadn't seen each other since Paula's birthday dinner and hadn't spoken on the phone for over a week.

"Kayla, are you there?"

"I'm here, yes. Here I am. Hello."

"Everything okay?"

"Sure, sure." I patted Flour's head so hard that she jumped down from my lap. "Sorry," I whispered to her.

"So, an old college buddy is in town," Jason said. "I think I might have mentioned him to you. Craig Houston."

"Of course. Craig. Craig Houston. How is good old Craig?" I slapped my forehead. What was wrong with me? It's like I didn't know how to have a conversation anymore.

"He's fine. He would like to meet you."

"Me? He'd like to meet me?"

"Kayla, are you all right? Should I call you another time?"

"No. This is fine. I'm fine. Craig Houston would like to meet me. That's good. I would also like to meet him."

"Are you free for dinner tonight or do you have something planned already? Could you come down to the restaurant?"

"Yes."

"Yes to what?" he asked. "Yes, you can come down to the restaurant?"

"Yes. I mean, right. I can come down to the restaurant tonight. No, I don't have anything planned."

"Great. Six-thirty?"

"Six-thirty is good. A good time. A good time for dinner, I mean." We hung up and I shook my head at myself. What in the world?

I pulled the weighted blanket over my legs and tried to decode why I was acting so frazzled. Besides the problems Jason and I had been experiencing lately, this was the first time I would meet someone significant to him besides his sister Paula. I knew Jason's nemesis, Leon, of course, but he was significant in a negative way.

I willed myself to stop thinking about it and shut myself in the kitchen to bake an order of cupcakes for a garden party. I dyed frosting with purple food gel and crafted ice plants, the county's favorite succulent, on top. As soon as the cupcakes were ready, I packed them up, and set out to deliver them to my client, Marian, on Whale Way. Marian, who wore a cute flowered jumpsuit with high-heeled pink sandals, led me out to the back garden and pointed to a picnic table. I laid out the cupcakes on the platter she'd provided and smiled at the guests in their spring dresses and floppy white hats. The weather was clear and mild, the perfect day to be enjoying the garden. Marian paid me and I went back home to relax.

ANXIETY FLARED UP IN MY CHEST as the time of dinner with Jason and Craig grew closer. I decided to bring in the big guns. I called Isabella. She agreed to bring over a selection of wardrobe choices and do my hair and makeup.

She came over a mere fifteen minutes later carrying a makeup bag and what looked like her entire closet draped over her arm.

"Whoa," I said.

"I know. But this time I won't make you wear contacts and I'll go easy on the makeup."

When Isabella had helped me get ready for my second date with Jason, she'd encouraged me to wear my contacts. She'd also made up my face so heavily that Jason didn't recognize me. I much preferred my glasses and a little mascara and lipstick.

We decided on a silky black tank and skinny jeans belonging to Isabella, a lightweight red sweater I located in my closet, and my trusty ballet flats. Isabella applied light makeup to my face and curled my hair.

I looked myself over in the bathroom mirror. "Okay, this is great, Iz. But I need some conversational help too. What in the heck do I talk about? You should have heard me on the phone with Jason. It was cringeworthy. And that was with him. What if that goes on tonight with Craig?"

"Just stick to the basics. Smile when you talk to him, look him in the eye."

"Only one eye?" I said and laughed.

"Do you want to impress this guy or not?" Isabella said sternly.

I got serious. "I do."

"You can ask him about his job. Encourage him to share what Jason was like in college. Talk about the ocean. The food. There's always the weather if you can't think of anything else."

I tried to keep everything in my head. "Thanks, Iz. I really do want his friend to like me." Maybe this would help Jason and me get back to where we used to be.

I STARTED OUT ON THE WRONG FOOT by getting my sweater caught on a post as I headed for the outdoor table where Jason and Craig were seated. At least I assumed it was Craig. The man sitting across from Jason could have been a movie star. He was incredibly good-looking and fit in an attractive white turtleneck sweater, the effect reminiscent of Robert Redford in *The Way We Were*.

I unhooked my sweater, patted down my hair, and approached the table. Jason had his back to me, and it took me stammering out a "hi" for him to turn around. He got up and enveloped me in a hug.

With his arm around me, he said to the man across the table, "This is Kayla. My one and only."

I was glad he felt that way despite all our recent problems.

"Craig, I presume?" *I presume?* I didn't talk like that. What was happening?

Craig stood, leaned over the table to shake my hand, and said, "It's a pleasure to meet you." He blinded me with a perfect smile.

"Good to meet you too." I congratulated myself for saying something articulate, if banal.

Jason patted the seat next to him and we sat down. I smiled at the two of them, my bottom lip trembling. What did Isabella say I should talk about? It had all disappeared from my head.

"I understand you're a baker," Craig said. "That is so cool."

"Yes. That's true. I mean, not that it's true that it's cool but it is true that I'm a baker. Well, I *do* think being a baker is cool. It's not that I don't." I threw Jason a "help me" look.

"We'll be having slices of her chocolate cake after dinner," Jason said.

"Terrific. My favorite," Craig said.

I bobbed my head up and down a few times.

"I'll go in and get our clam chowder," Jason said. "Is that good with you, Kayla?"

"Oh, sure. That's good. Anything is good. Whatever is easiest." Oh my god. He was going to leave me alone with Craig? My chest was so tight I wondered if I was too young to have a heart attack.

Jason left and I gave Craig a quivering smile. "What do you do, Craig?" That seemed fine. That was one of the safe topics, right?

He leaned forward across the table conspiratorially. "I'm an international man of mystery."

My mouth dropped open.

He laughed. "I'm kidding. I'm an accountant."

"Oh, right. Of course. Hey! My father is an accountant."

"So you know all the clichés about the job being dull. That's why I use the international man of mystery line."

"Yes. Okay." I told myself to shut up. His eyes were so blue. Even bluer than Jason's. Though the temperature was mild, I began to sweat. I took my sweater off and put it over the back of my seat.

Fortunately, Jason came back with our clam chowder in bread bowls a minute later. I dug in and willed myself to be normal. Sure, I was an introverted HSP, but I knew how to talk to people. I even interviewed possible murder suspects. Yes, Craig was gorgeous and yes, he was Jason's good friend. But he was just a person. A very cute person who was important to Jason. Ugh. I wished I could go home.

Jason and I reverted to our old standby of awkward dinner conversation.

"Are you enjoying the chowder, Kayla?" he asked.

"Yes, Jason, I really am."

"Would you like some oyster crackers?"

"Yes, I would. Thank you. That's nice of you. And thank you so much for the clam chowder."

When we moved on to dessert, a family with four kids came outside. They were making so much noise that I couldn't think straight. Jason kept glancing at me, picking up how bothered I was. I didn't want Craig to think poorly of me, so I acted as though I wasn't fazed. But I was becoming more and more overstimulated.

One of the children came up with a beach ball out of nowhere and tossed it into the air. The breeze off the water carried the ball over to our table and it bounced off my head. I'd had enough. I stood and shook Jason's hand, then went over to Craig and kissed him on the cheek. My face hot, I left.

I realized when I reached the mini-van that I'd forgotten my sweater. I went back. Jason and Craig were now at the deck rail, looking out at the ocean. I got closer so I could announce myself.

"Man, I just don't think she's the right one for you," Craig said, and I felt my chest tighten again.

I waited for Jason's response. When none was forthcoming, I left the sweater and retreated, my heart in a million pieces.

THE NEXT MORNING, STILL GOING NOWHERE with determining who Edward's killer was, and upset about the dinner with Jason and

Craig—I hadn't heard a word from Jason and I was too mortified to contact him—I was in a funk. I sipped listlessly on my coconut latte at the clubhouse restaurant, where I'd met Isabella during her break.

"It doesn't sound that bad," Isabella said after I told her about the dinner.

"Oh, yes, it was. Really, really bad. First of all, I was a nutcase."

"Didn't you tell me once you have a hard time performing in front of others?"

"That's true," I said. "But I wasn't getting a work evaluation. I was meeting Jason's friend."

"I think it's in the ballpark, sweetie. You shouldn't be so hard on yourself."

"Well, what about later? When Craig told Jason I'm not the right girl for him, and Jason said nothing. Nada. Zilch."

"I don't know, hon. I'm really sorry."

We were quiet until Isabella said, "Hey, do you want to do the 5K on Saturday? At the Founder's Festival?"

I blinked a few times at the change of subject.

"We don't have to run. We can walk," she said. "It's two miles around Alden Park and then out onto the walking path for the rest of the race."

"Sure. Why not?"

"And we'll go to lunch in the community room after?" Isabella asked gently.

"I guess so. If for no other reason, I want to find out what desserts they end up getting." And if they were as good as mine, but I didn't say it aloud.

I TOOK THE CATS OUT for another supervised excursion the next morning. Once more, Sugar nabbed a lizard and Flour was unsuccessful. They refused to come inside when I wanted them to, so I had to pick each one up by turn and take them into the house myself. I brought Flour onto my lap on the couch to try to assuage her feelings of failure, while Sugar did a celebratory run up and down the hallway.

A bit later, while I was sweeping the living room floor, my cell phone rang and Dad was on the other end. I filled him in on seeing Christie at the fast-food place.

"I'm stumped," I said. "I believed her when she said she didn't do it. I don't think it's Hugo. He doesn't seem to have it in him. Brenda doesn't make any sense because she won the competition. Maybe I really am the killer."

Dad laughed. "You know, one person we never gave much thought to is Conrad."

"Conrad? But why would *he* kill Edward?"

"I've been doing some digging of my own. There was a prior link between the two."

"Really?" Without looking, I lowered my backside onto the couch. Unfortunately, Flour was already there. She objected with a loud meow and jumped down.

"What's the link?" I asked Dad. "Conrad never mentioned anything."

"He dated Edward's mother the year before Edward was born. I uncovered a picture of the two at a big society event."

"Okay . . . wait, are you saying that Conrad might be Edward's father?"

"Exactly. What if Melody recently told Edward who his real father is? Edward might have applied for a guest chef position so he could get to Conrad. Perhaps he wanted a piece of the huge Cunningham fortune. Conrad already has several adult children and he might not have taken kindly to Edward trying to horn in. So, Conrad could have taken the opportunity of the power outage to get rid of him."

I thought that over for a few seconds and decided it was possible. "Wow. This puts a new spin on everything. Edward and Conrad were supposedly together for a while before dinner prep. This all could have come up."

"Right," Dad said. "Shall we go talk to Conrad?"

"Yes. I'm busy tomorrow, though. I'm going to the Founder's Festival here in the community."

"Have a good time. I'll pick you up on Sunday at ten?"

I said that was fine and we hung up.

PART OF ME HOPED IT WOULD RAIN on the day of the Founder's Festival because the board of directors had cancelled my contract. It was a small-minded wish I reprimanded myself for. I didn't want anyone to be disappointed. I'd run into Angie and Vicky on the coastal path after I'd talked to my dad the day before, and Angie was looking forward to it. As a young introverted HSP, she wasn't particularly interested in parties, but she *was* into party food, especially desserts, and who could blame her?

The day opened with a light cloud cover that cleared by nine-thirty, half an hour before the start of the race. No signs of rain.

I met Isabella in the center of Alden Park, where the 5K would begin. Giggling to ourselves, we copied the runners by doing a few stretches and jogging in place.

"Is Brian doing the race?" I asked. "Or does he have to work?"

"He's off today, but he's getting his hair cut at ten. He's coming after to check out the party."

"Kayla!" a voice called. I turned toward the sound and saw Stella, the grandmother of Brian's partner, Lisa, waving to me. She walked over with her dog, Beau. I'd taken care of the elderly yellow Lab for a brief time in December and hadn't laid eyes on him since Stella adopted him. I was delighted by the unexpected meeting.

Stella had pulled her white hair back into a ponytail. Her lively blue eyes crinkled as she smiled at us. The pleasant scent of her floral perfume wafted over to me.

"Well, hello," I said, giving Stella a brief hug and bending down to pat Beau. He seemed to remember me and barked a couple of times in greeting.

I straightened up and pointed to Isabella. "Stella, do you know Isabella Valera?"

"Isabella, I've heard so much about you. Your beau talks to my granddaughter about you all the time." Stella clapped her hand over her mouth. "Oh, my. I shouldn't have said anything. It's not as though everyone's gossiping about you, dear."

Isabella placed her hand on Stella's. "It's fine. It's good to know that Brian talks about me."

"Oh, yes. He does constantly, from what I understand. He's so impressed that you're planning to go to law school and will become a women's rights attorney. I'm very impressed as well."

Isabella's face lit up with pleasure.

"How is Beau doing?" I asked. "He looks great."

"Got the all-clear on his physical a couple of weeks ago. We're the best of friends. I get along better with him than with some members of my own family." Stella laughed.

"I'm glad it's worked out," I said. "Are you guys doing the 5K?"

"It's a little far for us. But we're here to support everyone who's walking and running."

"That's really nice," I said. "Please say hello to Lisa for us."

Isabella winked at Stella. "Yes. And please tell her to encourage Brian to keep talking about me."

Stella winked back. "Of course. Good luck, dears."

I leaned down to give Beau another pat. "Take care, sweetie." I'd considered keeping him back in December, but I had my hands full with the cats . . . and two murders to solve. It was good to see him.

We next ran into Eileen Nichols, a neighbor of my late friend, Trudy. Isabella and I said hello and asked her how she was.

"Fine. Still missing Trudy a lot."

"I understand," I said. "Me too."

"How are the cats?" Eileen had taken care of Sugar the night after Trudy's death but had been unable to keep the cat because of her allergies. She always asked after both Sugar and Flour.

"They're terrific."

"I saw you on the news," Eileen said. "What's this about another murder? You're a magnet for dead bodies." Her face fell when she saw my expression. "Oh, I didn't mean it like that. I'm sorry."

"It's all right," I said. "It does seem that way."

Before we could talk more, Freida Jimenez from the community's board of directors called everyone over to the start line by blowing on a whistle—a noise I did not approve of at all.

I said good-bye to Eileen, and Isabella and I lined up next to the other walkers.

"You okay?" Isabella asked. "Eileen wasn't too tactful back there."

"I'm okay. It's true, right? Bodies all over the place."

"Try not to think about it. Let's enjoy ourselves."

Freida blew the whistle again and we started walking.

We went at a good pace, talking about anything that struck our fancy, with a few exceptions. We didn't discuss the murder or my issues with Jason. Isabella entertained me with stories of her trip to Vegas, which had me laughing.

"So, get this," she said. "Brian had two cocktails before dinner on our last night. He was swaying around the hotel room, telling me how much he loves me. Then he fell over and went to sleep. We never made it to dinner."

"That's actually rather sweet," I said, picturing serious police detective Brian gushing over how much he loved my best friend. Not having much to compete with that story, I told her about the cats' excursions out to the patio and Flour's run of bad luck.

We circled around the park. I pointed out to Isabella where the Oceanville Playworld merry-go-round once stood, based on its location in Tristan's painting.

When something interested me, I tended to go overboard with finding out everything I could. Isabella was indulgent with me as I told her what I'd seen at the museum and the things I'd discovered on the internet when I'd done more research later.

"It sounds really neat, sweetie," Isabella said nicely, but her eyes were glazing over. I switched the topic to her law school admission exam. She was both nervous and excited to take it that coming summer. She told me that in addition to studying, she was looking into scholarships to help pay for tuition.

After circling the park, we followed the crowd onto the coastal walk and went about half a mile before turning around. When we passed the finish line back at Alden Park, I felt relaxed and refreshed. I made a mental note to take to the trail more.

Freida gave out the awards, trophies presumably shaped in Theresa Alden's image, though the rather big head had Isabella and me smiling. Cat Chiu, the founder of Seaside Shores's popular book club, won for the women, and Austin Williams took first place for the men. I was happy for them both, despite Austin cancelling my contract for his anniversary party, and Isabella and I cheered and hollered in appreciation.

My upbeat mood evaporated once Isabella and I had strolled over to the community offices after the awards ceremony. Despite my smiles, people were bypassing me right and left in the community room, people whom I'd thought of as not just clients but as friends. No one was making eye contact.

"I can't believe this, Iz," I said. "After Stella and Eileen, no one's said hello to me. I'm a pariah."

"I'm sure that's not true," Isabella said, taking a sip of the signature drink for the event, a peach and cherry lemonade the organizing committee had dubbed Alden-ade.

"Then explain why no one has come to speak to us," I said.

She looked around and then back at me. "I see what you mean."

"I'm gonna go look at the desserts." And leave after, I thought.

The desserts, spread out across three folding tables, were enchanting. Icings had incorporated a spring theme by adding sugar flowers to different-flavored cupcakes and filling butterfly-shaped cookie cups with lemon curd. I piled a few treats on a plate and nibbled on a cookie cup, which was quite tasty. Were the desserts better than mine would have been? Maybe.

I was feeling awfully sorry for myself when Jason's sister Paula approached.

"Paula. I'm so glad to see someone who actually wants to talk to me, possible murder suspect that I am."

She gave me a hug. "I can't be the only one."

I smiled. "Well, when Angie and Vicky get here, no."

"I don't think they're coming. I saw Vicky on the trail early this morning and she said Angie's not feeling well. And, honestly, I've had enough interaction for today. I'm gonna head out."

"HSP moment?" I asked. She nodded and we said good-bye.

I tried to catch Isabella's eye, but Brian had arrived. He kissed her cheek and whispered in her ear. They stepped aside to look at the photo exhibit, which told the story of the planning and building of Seaside Shores. That was my cue. I left.

AT HOME, I REVIEWED THE RECENT EVENTS in my life, none of them good. I flopped onto the couch and cuddled up with Sugar and Flour.

"It's been a rough few weeks," I said to them. "But I did get to spend time with my dad. He and I are getting along well now. That, my friends, is a very good thing."

CHAPTER 11

T HE NEXT MORNING, I WAS THRILLED TO READ in the local paper that Jason's chowder had been named the best in Ocean County following National Clam Chowder Day at the end of February. I immediately called to congratulate him but couldn't get through. I left a message.

I walked down to the clubhouse restaurant to see how Vincent had progressed on his latest pie homework. He handed me a decaf vanilla latte and unveiled a chocolate cream pie. Although the crust was fine this time, he'd overwhipped the cream. I told him as gently as I could.

"It's okay, Vincent. You're going to get this." I patted his back.

"Are you sure?"

"Yes. I'm positive. Keep practicing and I'll see you soon, all right, for our cheesecake lesson? Thursday next week?"

He nodded.

I left, thinking how I'd misjudged Vincent. Before I began teaching him, I thought him grumpy and difficult. In truth, he was a big teddy bear who only wanted to bake and be good at it. I told myself I'd ramp up my efforts to help him achieve his dream.

DAD PICKED ME UP SOON AFTERWARD for our drive over to The Countryside Inn to talk to Conrad. Was Dad right that Conrad was Edward's father? Would Conrad have killed his own son to keep him away from the family's substantial fortune? It was hard to believe, but humans sometimes did inconceivable and evil things when money was involved.

There wasn't much traffic and we arrived in no time. We parked in the lot and walked toward the hotel. Was I imagining it or did the regal inn look diminished after the tragedy? Even the art deco ceiling in the lobby seemed less impressive than when I'd first seen it.

We asked the front desk clerk if we could talk to Conrad. He made a call and pointed the way to the hotel offices. "He's in the second office to the left," he said.

Conrad called for us to come in when we knocked on his open door. In contrast to his immaculate office, Conrad looked like he'd been run over by a truck, in even worse shape than we'd seen him last.

"Hi, Conrad," I said. "How are you feeling?"

"Been better. What can I do for you?"

"The memorial was nice, wasn't it?" I asked.

"As memorials go, sure." The effort to answer my question appeared to exhaust him and his shoulders slumped. He looked down at his desk.

Dad gestured at me to go ahead.

"I didn't realize you knew Melody, Edward's mother," I said.

This perked him up and his eyes bore into mine.

"The two of you dated, didn't you?" Dad said. "About thirty-five, thirty-six years ago?"

"What are you getting at?" The rancor behind his words made us back up a couple of steps.

I said as neutrally as I could, "We just wondered, well, if it's possible that Edward was your son?"

He leapt to his feet and stormed around the desk to us. "I think you'd better leave now." We beat a hasty retreat.

Back in the car, I said to Dad, "Either he didn't appreciate us asking about personal matters, or we hit a nerve and were right in our accusations. I don't know which. But it was scary."

"I don't think we'd better talk to him again about this. But there *is* another way to go about it."

"What's that?" I asked.

"We could talk to Edward's mother, Melody."

"Do you think she'll tell us the truth?"

"Only one way to find out."

"Okay. Let's go see her tomorrow," I said. "If nothing else, we'll finally be able to give her our condolences."

THE NEXT MORNING, I PICKED UP DAD and we drove to La Tierra to Edward's mother's house, where we'd attended the memorial service. We rang the doorbell twice, but there was no answer.

We walked over to the back gate and I called out, "Hello? Melody, are you in there?"

"Yes, I'm in here," a voice said. "Come in."

Dad undid the latch and we went through to the backyard. Melody, wearing jeans and a flowered gardening apron over a short-sleeved shirt, was using a trowel to scoop dirt into a small pot.

"Hello," she said, putting the trowel down and removing her gardening gloves. "I remember you two. You were at the service, weren't you?"

Her red eyes revealed she'd recently been crying and I felt a pang of sympathy. No one at the memorial service had identified themselves as Edward's sibling and I guessed he'd had no brothers or sisters. How awful that Melody had lost her only child. I hadn't been aware of Edward's father at the service, either, and wondered if she was a widow. If so, she had no one in the house to share her grief.

"Yes, we were there," I said. "I'm Kayla Jeffries and this is my father, Andrew. We're so sorry for your loss. We're wondering if we could talk to you for a minute?" Would she recognize my name from the news and kick us out?

"Of course. It's nice to have company. Why don't you sit at the table and I'll get us drinks. Do you like root beer?"

Dad and I nodded.

She pointed to a picnic table in the shadow of an orange tree and we sat. The garden looked lovely, with camellias and geraniums in bloom. I was glad Melody was keeping herself busy, though I hoped she was allowing herself time to grieve. I'd lost two very important people in my life: my grandmother and my friend, Trudy. My grandmother died of natural causes, but, like Edward, Trudy's life had been taken from her. That added to the depth of the grief, at least for me, and I knew how vital it was not to push the bad feelings away.

When Melody came back with the drinks, we told her how nice the garden looked. She thanked us and sat at the table next to Dad.

"I enjoy it," she said, looking around. "Especially now. I feel I have to keep myself busy or I'll break down." She wiped a tear from her eye, and I patted her hand across the table. "Now what did you want to talk to me about?"

I didn't want to upset her since she was already in a fragile state. I said carefully, "I don't know if you're aware of this, but I was in the kitchen when Edward was . . . hurt. The police have been questioning me. It's possible I'm a suspect."

She drew back, surprised. "Surely not."

"It's true. But I didn't hurt your son, I promise. We're trying to work out who did, though. The police haven't gotten very far." I took a sip of root beer.

"They've talked to me several times, and that's the feeling I got, as well," Melody said. "I'm not sure it matters to me anymore. Finding the killer won't bring him back."

"Yes. But the person should be brought to justice," Dad said.

She looked away once more toward the garden. "I suppose so. But I don't see how I can help you. I've told the police everything I know." She returned her attention to me. "You said your name is Kayla? You're the college girlfriend the police asked me about, aren't you?"

"Edward and I went to UC Springvale at the same time, but we didn't know each other," I said. "I wasn't his girlfriend by any stretch of the imagination. That whole thing was a case of mistaken identity."

"I see. Yes, I told them I remembered a girlfriend from college, but I didn't recall if Kayla was her name. I never met her."

"Kaycee Jeffs was his girlfriend."

"Yes, that's it. I remember now. The police also asked me about a recent girlfriend. Christie. I met her once, but I didn't feel she and Edward were the best match. They didn't seem to like each other much. I wish my Ted had had the chance to find someone special."

"I'm sorry. I wish that too," I said. "Melody, what we wanted to ask you about is, well, somewhat delicate."

"Delicate?"

"It's about Conrad Cunningham, the owner of The Countryside Inn. You knew him a number of years ago?"

"Oh, yes, I did know him, but we haven't been in contact for many years. When Edward told me he was going to be cooking at The Countryside, I mentioned to him that I knew Conrad long ago. Edward invited me to the hotel for the weekend, but I already had plans. Maybe if I'd been there . . ."

"I don't think it would have made a difference," I said, touching her hand again.

"I'm sure you're right. I saw Conrad at the service, but he ducked out before I could speak to him."

"You knew him around the time of Edward's birth?" Dad asked.

"Well, yes. Why?" Her shrewd eyes looked us over. "Conrad and I didn't date. We were friends, that's all. My husband, Allen, was quite ill his entire life. He encouraged me to not stay at home with him all the time. He wanted me to have fun. I met Conrad at an art exhibition, and we hit it off. His wife didn't like going out, so Conrad and I spent time together. We liked the same artwork and restaurants, so we went to museums and out to eat a few times a month."

"So . . . there's no chance that..." I said, trailing off.

"Conrad wasn't Edward's father, no," she said. "But . . . neither was Allen. He couldn't have children."

"We're sorry to overstep," Dad said.

"I did have an affair." Melody looked down at the table. "I'm not proud of it. But it wasn't with Conrad. No, it was someone else, and if you don't mind, I'd like to protect his privacy."

"Of course," I said. "But is it possible Edward *thought* Conrad was his father?"

"No. And Edward never really knew Conrad. They met once, I think, but Edward was young. I told him the identity of his real father when he turned eighteen. I said it was fine with me if he wanted to pursue a relationship with this person, but Edward strongly felt my late husband was his true father. Allen raised him and was glad to. We were a happy family. Allen forgave me for the affair."

So that was that.

"Thank you, Melody," I said as Dad and I got up from the table. "Again, we're so sorry about Edward. And your husband too."

"Thank *you*, Kayla. I hope things work out for you. You're both very nice."

On the way to the car, I decided I'd bake something special for Melody and deliver it soon. Perhaps some of the raspberry cream cupcakes. They were so pretty, and tasty too.

When I dropped Dad off at the hotel, he said before he went inside, "Honey, I have to go back to Florida for a couple of days to attend to something at work. Call if you need me. Any time of day or night. I've asked the hotel to hang onto my room. I'll be back before you know it."

"Okay. Sure. Good luck, Dad." As I drove off, I realized I still hadn't shown him the cottage. I would have him over for dinner as soon as he returned from Florida.

THE ISSUE OF THE STOLEN NAPKIN from Scales and Fins had been weighing on me for a while now. I'd left it on my dresser, and every time I walked past, I felt a stab of regret. I reached a decision. I would return the napkin to Leon and apologize. It was the right thing to do and would alleviate my feelings of guilt.

The following afternoon, I retrieved the napkin from the dresser, rounded up a few dirty towels, and went to my closet where my stacked washer/dryer lived. Ninety minutes later, when the napkin was fresh from the dryer, I unearthed my iron and gently smoothed out the wrinkles.

I drove the mini-van to Scales and Fins and asked the hostess if I could speak to Leon. It was 2:30, between lunch and dinner, so only a few customers were seated in the dining room. The hostess gave me an odd look when she saw the napkin in my hand but agreed to find her boss. While she was gone, I admired the fish swimming through the lighted indoor waterways. The waterways were a popular feature of the restaurant and were often pictured in tourist brochures.

Leon came into the room a few minutes later.

I cleared my throat and handed him the napkin. "I took this by accident and am returning it to you. It's been washed and ironed. I apologize for the mistake." I wanted to underscore the point that I hadn't meant to take the napkin and wasn't knowingly a thief.

He frowned. "Is that all?"

"Yes, that's all." What else did he want?

"You lied about who you were."

I nodded to acknowledge the truth of his statement. "I apologize for that as well. I was trying to work out who had killed my friend. My very good friend. It's not something I would normally do, but the circumstances were . . . dire."

The idea that I'd been trying to suss him out as a potential killer must not have occurred to him before. His face turned bright red. He blustered, "What? You're saying you thought I was a murderer?"

The couple at a table nearby turned to stare.

Keeping my voice low, I said, "I was only eliminating people. I didn't really suspect you." This, of course, was a lie and did little to restore my credibility.

"I suggest you leave now," he said, and I decided that was a good idea.

As I held the door open for a family coming into the restaurant, I turned back. Leon held my gaze and stuffed the napkin into the little trash can behind the hostess stand.

ISABELLA CAME OVER THAT EVENING and we ordered in Mexican food—burritos, tostadas, and guacamole and chips. I told her about the visit to Leon and asked what she had been doing.

"I've been studying all day. I'm exhausted but it's going well," she said, chewing on a chip. "Which isn't to say it's not hard."

I took a bite of burrito and wiped my mouth with a napkin. "You're gonna do great."

"I've been practicing logic puzzles. Didn't you say you've been using a logic puzzle to solve your murder?"

I gaped at her. "*My* murder?"

"Sorry. Bad phrasing. *The* murder, then."

"Yeah, it's kind of like a logic puzzle but it's not really the same." I found my grid and showed it to her, explaining that it was simplified because I was able to leave out means and opportunity.

"So you don't think this guy did it?" she asked, pointing to Hugo's name. The night before, I'd added a new column to the grid that described how believable I'd found each suspect to be after talking with them. I'd penciled in that both Hugo and Christie had come off credibly.

"Not that the killer couldn't be a woman," Isabella went on, "but the method strikes me as more of a masculine act, don't you think? Stabbing someone with a pair of shears in the back of the neck?"

I considered this. "I know what you mean. But you should see him, Iz. He's young and has a cowlick and comes off so innocent. He's clumsy. He says 'dude' and 'bullpucky.' He just doesn't appear to have what it takes to kill someone in cold blood."

"And the two women do?"

"I don't know. I really don't. Brenda doesn't have a solid motive, because she won *Premier Chef* over Edward instead of the other way around. Christie potentially *does* have a motive because she'd been involved with Edward and had at least one fight with him I know of. Plus, she was awfully irritable during dinner prep. Maybe she was upset to see Edward and that boiled over."

"But you're not convinced?"

"She seemed sincere when I spoke with her. She denied killing him. But, no, I'm not convinced. What do you think?"

Isabella shook her head. "I think studying for the LSAT isn't so bad, after all. Pass the guacamole."

I did as she said.

THE NEXT EVENING, I WAS SCHEDULED to have dinner with Tristan and Jeremy at Sam's. We'd finally found a time to get together. Before I left to meet them at the restaurant, I had a typical introvert reaction when faced with the prospect of going out. I would have preferred to stay at home with the cats and a book. I looked at the phone, hoping one of them would call to cancel. It stubbornly remained silent.

But Tristan was a good friend, and although I didn't know Jeremy very well yet, I liked him a lot. So I rallied and walked down to the wharf.

At Sam's, the two greeted me warmly and we took a table on the deck. We asked for oysters to start and several seafood entrees to share. As we dug into the oysters, we talked easily about art and cooking, laughing a lot.

Then Tristan said, "Any news on the murder? Have you figured out the killer yet?"

"About that. Can I run something by you guys?"

"Let's hear it," Jeremy said. He offered me another oyster, which I accepted.

I slurped up the oyster and said, "The kitchen manager was on *Premier Chef* with the victim. I can't get over the feeling that that has something to do with the murder. But I can't find the proof. And the kitchen manager won, so it doesn't make much sense."

"Never saw it," Jeremy said. "But I watched *Master Painter* religiously."

"Oooh, I loved that show," Tristan said. "They cancelled it after only one season. I was so sad. I had my application all ready for season two."

Jeremy said, "You would have been perfect, T. I read an article about the show later. Apparently, there was a lot of creative editing. The producers embellished disagreements, made it seem like contestants were having relationships when they weren't—that kind of thing. That ruined the whole experience for me."

"I've heard that about reality shows," I said, wondering if something similar on *Premier Chef* might tie in with the hotel murder. When I voiced my thought, Tristan and Jeremy encouraged me to look into it.

Our entrees arrived and the subject changed. Tristan said there was a documentary of Oceanville Playworld he was trying to get ahold of and invited me to watch it with him. Of course, I agreed. We each shared some new information we'd found out about the park. Jeremy humored us, though I felt he wasn't as interested as we were.

The three of us devoured the red snapper, filet of sole, and shrimp salad. My shoulders relaxed and my mood lifted. The evening was mild, the water a tranquil blue under the moonlight, the company pleasant. As I looked out to the ocean, I felt extremely grateful to live where I did and to have such good friends.

After the meal, Jeremy and Tristan offered to drive me home and I accepted. Jeremy told knock-knock jokes all the way to my cottage. The jokes were corny, but Jeremy's serious delivery was hilarious. The three of us bid each other a fond good-night.

THE NEXT MORNING, AFTER I DELIVERED a whale-shaped cake to a marine biologist's retirement party, I lay down on the couch to relax. The cats came running, knowing with some sixth sense that I was available for cuddles.

Flour got to me before Sugar and sprawled across my chest. I stroked her gently and she lifted her head for chin scratches. She wiggled around in ecstasy and pushed her paws back and forth. Sugar, pretending she didn't care, left the room. Flour, perhaps thinking Sugar knew something she didn't, jumped down to the floor. Now that I was unencumbered, I sat up, thinking once again about Edward's murder. Who the heck had done it?

I knew *I* wasn't the killer. I didn't think Hugo was capable of it. He couldn't even take hand pies off a baking sheet without dropping one. Christie had come off believably when I talked to her. Melody confirmed that Conrad wasn't Edward's father, so I couldn't think of a reason for the billionaire to be the murderer. I hadn't even put him on my grid. That only left Brenda. It couldn't be coincidence that she and Edward had been on a televised competition together, could it? Even though *Premier Chef* wasn't the most well-known cooking show, it was still broadcast on national TV and offered substantial prize money. Surely there was a motive there.

Remembering what Jeremy had said about the editing on *Master Painter*, I decided to watch the *Premier Chef* episodes again, more closely this time, on TV. My free trial for the streaming service was valid for a while longer, so I set it up.

Nothing unusual jumped out at me at first, other than the fact that Brenda, the eventual winner, didn't capture any of the wins for the main challenges in the first three episodes and was even in the bottom two contestants each time. For those three episodes, she eventually squeaked by and wasn't eliminated.

And then I saw her put way too much salt into her pie crust in the fourth episode centered on desserts, just like Vincent had done with his first attempt at making one. It would have been easy to miss; a layperson might not have caught it. I was always extremely careful with my salt so I picked up on it.

By the time Brenda presented her dish, the judges were falling all over her, praising her and giving her compliments.

Doug Terwilliger called it the best dessert he'd ever tasted. Terry Wilson said he'd pay twenty dollars for it at a restaurant. Samantha Nawakura described it as sublime.

What was going on here?

CHAPTER 12

I WANTED TO TALK TO DAD, BUT when I called him, I was immediately put through to voice mail. I hung up without leaving a message.

Isabella wasn't available, either. I remembered her telling me that the restaurant was holding a private event today. Vincent had forbidden her to have her phone on.

I chewed on my fingernail and looked at the cats, who were now cuddled up together at the end of the couch. Did I have the guts to talk to Jason? Not really, but I'd go anyway.

In the wharf parking lot, I circled around and finally found someone pulling out of a space. I paid for a ticket for the windshield and walked down the crowded wharf. Tourists streamed in and out of shops and stopped at restaurants to read menus. A long line had formed for a whale watching tour and I had to weave in and out of the queue, all the while wishing I were free of all worries and could go along.

Jason was delivering an order to a table when I walked into Fishes Do Come True. He came over to me once he was done.

"Hey, best chowder," I said, hugging him. "Congratulations."

"Thank you." He looked at me expectantly. I fondly remembered the days when I could visit him *just because*, and not get a look asking what the heck I was doing there.

"I had to tell someone. I found something out," I said.

"Okay. Shoot."

"Brenda put way too much salt in her pie crust. And she won the competition."

"I'm sorry?"

"The judges said they *liked* it. Not just liked it but *loved* it."

"I'm still not following, Kayla."

I explained about *Premier Chef*. "There's no way that tasted good. I think the whole thing was rigged. It's not uncommon for reality shows to be edited in certain ways, but this is on a different level. I mean, sure, they might do an alternate take or play up a conflict, like Jeremy told me, but nothing as egregious as this."

"Let me catch up here. Are you saying this ties into the murder somehow?"

"Yes. I think Edward was going to expose her. Brenda should have been eliminated early on. *He* was the rightful winner. But for some reason the producers wanted Brenda to win. I think Brenda had to kill him before he did anything about it." I left out the conundrum of Brenda not knowing the windstorm would knock the power out. I hadn't worked that part out yet.

Jason took a few seconds to absorb this. He appeared to come to the decision to take me seriously and said, "Okay. So you'll tell the lead detective?"

I bit my lip and avoided his gaze.

"You're not going to talk to this woman by yourself, are you?"

"No. Of course not. That would be . . . dangerous."

Jason's sous chef, Timothy, came into the dining room and asked for help in the kitchen.

"Give me a second," Jason said to him before turning back to me. "Kayla?"

"Go ahead," I said. "I'll be fine. Don't worry."

I DROVE HOME, THINKING OVER THE CONVERSATION with Jason. If I did as he wanted and went to the police station, Det. Hernandez would dismiss my theory out of hand. At no point had he even considered Brenda.

No, I would have to confront her myself and tell her what I'd found out. But I'd talk to her while she was at work so I wouldn't be alone with her. If she *was* the murderer, she could hardly hurt me in public.

I finally reached Dad and told him my theory and my plan to talk to Brenda.

"I just got back in town to the hotel. Do you want some company?" he asked.

"Always."

"Let me quickly put my things away. What time should I pick you up? Or do you want to drive?"

"I'll pick you up. Is ten minutes too soon?"

"That's fine. I'll be outside, bright-eyed and bushy-tailed. Or perhaps I should say with my Poirot mustache finely groomed?"

I laughed. I hung up, happy that my father was going with me. What a difference a few weeks had made. At The Countryside that first day, I couldn't wait to get away from him.

Ten minutes later, we took off in the mini-van for Los Robles once again.

I caught Dad up with what I'd been doing. Then I glanced over and said, "Everything okay with work?"

He pushed his glasses back onto his nose. They were loose again. "Not great. I've been going through a late mid-life crisis, I suppose," he said. "My attitude at work began to be a problem, so the partners and I agreed I would take some time away. I've been off work since the beginning of the year. Unpaid."

He could have knocked me over with a feather. Attitude problems? I never would have guessed.

"And . . . being with you and talking to you has made me yearn to follow my dreams of becoming an artist."

I was so shocked that I drifted into the lane next to us. I quickly corrected. "I never knew you were interested in doing that."

"I've wanted to explore art my whole life, but I was always too tired from work to pursue it. Or perhaps I was scared. If you never try, you can't fail, right?"

"Wow."

"You inspired me, K-Bear. I went home to resign."

"Dad, that's incredible. I'm so impressed."

"Well, thank you. I certainly hope it's the right decision. Stacy isn't completely onboard."

"Why not?"

"She's worried about our long-term plans. She was already concerned that I was having time off without pay and now . . . she's not sure about me leaving the job permanently. We'd talked about traveling around the world and then settling in London, which of course would be expensive. Resigning might not be a wise move, but it feels like the right one."

"I'm proud of you. And if Stacy can't deal, she isn't the right woman."

"Thank you, honey."

I bit the bullet and confessed to him that Jason and I also weren't doing well. I told him about the dinner at Paula's and the invitation to the mountains I had to turn down, as well as the unfortunate dinner with Craig. Dad expressed his sympathy.

"We're a couple of sad sacks, aren't we?" Dad said, and we laughed. At least we were in the same boat.

WE ARRIVED AT THE COUNTRYSIDE INN twenty minutes later. The parking lot was nearly empty.

"I guess business hasn't picked up yet," Dad mused.

"Poor Conrad."

We went into the restaurant and asked one of the waiters if Brenda was around. As luck would have it, she had the day off. The waiter recommended we get her contact information from Conrad, so we headed for his office.

He invited us in and we told him we were hoping to talk to Brenda.

"We're not even at half capacity," he said. "The restaurant hasn't exactly been bustling, so I gave her time off."

At our request, he reluctantly gave us Brenda's home address, which was nearby to the hotel. She had relocated from Los Angeles to Los Robles when he hired her, he said.

"I certainly hope she's not the killer," he said to me. "Frankly, I was hanging my hat on you being the one. We didn't technically hire you. We hired Amanda and you took over. And then you came around asking personal questions . . ." He trailed off.

"It's not me," I said. "I promise. But we *are* sorry for the intrusive questions the other day. We know the score now."

He looked contrite. "I shouldn't have said that. I'm not myself. I'm constantly worried the hotel is finished."

I knew the feeling, unfortunately recalling all the cancellations I'd sustained lately.

"I bet things will pick up," I said. "Once the killer is apprehended, things will calm down and people will start booking again." Maybe it was true; it was the same thing I said to myself when I was worried about my own business. He thanked me and we left.

As we went through the lobby to leave the hotel, Dad said, "Have you thought of asking Conrad if he'd like to order desserts from you? Assuming the hotel survives?"

"They have a famous pastry chef on their regular staff," I told him. "I saw it on the website. But thanks. That's nice of you to think of that."

"You're very talented. Everyone should have the chance to try your desserts."

"Thanks, Dad. That means a lot."

He smiled and we walked to the car.

AFTER WE CLEARED THE LONG ROAD that serviced the hotel, Dad said, "Perhaps we should let Detective Hernandez know what we're thinking and doing. For safety reasons. In case Brenda *is* the killer."

"I doubt he'll take us seriously but I think you're right. And that will settle my conscience for not telling Jason the full truth."

We drove to the police station and after getting the okay, headed for Det. Hernandez's office.

When we walked in the door, he closed his eyes, put his hand to his temple, and shook his head. "What now? Are you finally confessing?"

"No," I said. "As I've told you all along, I'm not guilty. But I know who is."

Now he put his head down to his desk. Voice muffled, he said, "Please help me understand, Ms. Jeffries, how you could have solved this case when people trained many years to do so have not."

I explained my whole theory to him.

He let a number of seconds go by before lifting his head and saying, "Let me get this straight. Because she put too much of an ingredient in a dessert, she's a killer?"

"You have to admit it's fishy," I said. "I think Edward was going to expose her as a fraud. He was the rightful winner. To stop that from happening, she killed him."

He got up from his chair, apparently wanting to end the meeting. "You're a baker, are you not?"

"Yes. Why?"

"You might want to look into writing. You're really quite good at making up stories."

"It's not a story. Watch the episode. You'll see. She put in too much salt, which would have ruined her dessert, and the judges said they liked it."

He shrugged. "Perhaps you missed the part where she realized her mistake and started over. Or they edited it out."

"No, I don't think so. There wasn't enough time for her to start over. The clock was shown several times during the challenge. I believe the producers wanted Brenda to win for some reason."

He looked back at me, unmoved.

"You admitted that no one has solved the case yet. You could go talk to her at least," I said, still trying to get something—anything—from him.

"If you're right, and she wanted to kill Edward so this wouldn't come out, why didn't she have it planned better? She couldn't have known the power would go out."

"Maybe her first method didn't work, so when the lights went out, she improvised. Or, what about this? He could have only just told her before the power went out that he was going to expose her. When the room went dark, she seized the opportunity."

He shook his head. "Remember what I said? Facts, Ms. Jeffries. We deal in facts. You have a good trip home."

We left.

OUT ON THE SIDEWALK, I turned to Dad. "Any ideas?"

"I think we should follow the original plan and talk to Brenda," he said. "We'll have safety in numbers if she is the killer."

We followed the directions Conrad had provided and arrived at Brenda's house ten minutes later. Dad rang the bell.

Brenda answered the door right away, looking as though she was expecting someone.

"Hi, Brenda. How are you?" I said.

"What are you doing here?" she asked me. She looked at Dad. "Who are you?"

I said, "This is my father, Andrew. We were just at the hotel and Conrad mentioned you lived here. So we thought we'd stop by and see how you're doing."

"He gave you my address?"

Without answering her question, I said, "Can we come in for a minute? We won't be long. That whole murder thing was so stressful. It would be good to talk to someone else who went through it. That was crazy, right? A murder right in front of us?"

She held the door open and we went in.

"May I have a glass of water?" I asked.

She led us to the kitchen and got a pitcher out of the fridge. She retrieved three glasses from the cupboard.

How to proceed? I decided to flatter her first. "I saw the *Premier Chef* episodes. That is so cool. Congrats. You won."

"Thanks." She shifted her weight from one foot to the other as she started pouring water into a glass. She seemed inpatient for this conversation to get underway.

"What happened in the fourth episode?" I said, leaning in confidentially. "You put too much salt in your crust, right?"

"I don't know what you mean."

"You made a mistake, didn't you?" Dad said.

She froze in the middle of filling the glass. "Look, I'm not supposed to be talking about this. We all signed NDAs. Non-disclosure agreements. Can you promise this will stay between us?"

"Of course," I said while Dad nodded.

She finished pouring the water and handed me the glass. She prepared another and held it up to Dad. He shook his head, so she claimed it for herself and took a long sip. "You've got to understand that this was a new show on a lesser-known cable channel. The producers had a hard time attracting top-flight chefs despite the good prize money. Most of us hadn't won awards or owned restaurants."

"Right," I said. "I see."

"For some reason, I was popular with viewers, but I'm not that great a chef. Edward was the standout, much more talented than the rest of us. But the fans hated him. And not in a 'love to hate him' kind of way. He was arrogant and rude to the judges, refusing to take constructive criticism. The producers were worried the show wouldn't be renewed if he won. The fans would be mad and might not tune in for another season. So . . . they kept me on and eventually made me the winner."

"I'm guessing Edward was going to break his NDA and go public with that?" I said. "Is that why you killed him?"

She gave me a blank look. Then she laughed and couldn't stop. She doubled over, laughing.

Dad and I looked at each other, flummoxed.

"What? Why is it funny?" I watched Brenda continue to laugh, practically falling into hysterics. This was not going at all the way I expected.

"Kill him?" she said. "I didn't kill him. Sure, he was upset about not being crowned the winner, mostly because of his oversized ego, but it didn't bother him all that much. They paid him as though he'd won. And his restaurant got even more successful after."

I didn't think she was lying. "I'm sorry. I shouldn't have accused you."

"No skin off my nose."

"Do you have any theories on who did kill him?" Dad asked.

She shook her head. "No. I don't. And I've thought about it a lot. I'm sorry, but I'm expecting someone. I have to get going."

"Thanks for seeing us," Dad said. "We'll let ourselves out."

"You might not be the best chef, but you're a great manager," I said as we exited the kitchen. "You were so calm and collected after Edward was stabbed and you knew exactly what to do. It was impressive."

She nodded to acknowledge the compliment.

Dad said as we got in the car, "Well? Now what? I believe her. Do you?"

"I do. I was really off about that. And now . . . I have no clue where to go next."

"Neither do I."

"How about dinner later? My place," I said. "It's about time I show you the cottage. Of course, when I say dinner, I mean pizza. And when I say pizza, I mean the kind you order online and have delivered."

"I'd love to."

"Maybe we'll have some ideas by then."

CHAPTER 13

WHEN DAD ARRIVED AT SEVEN FOR DINNER, he handed me a present wrapped in newspaper, with a shoelace for a bow.

"Sorry, I forgot to pick up wrapping paper," he said. "Had to use the newspaper they left outside my door at the hotel."

"A present? That's so nice. What for?"

"Well, this is my first visit to your cottage. Consider it a housewarming present. Better late than never."

I thanked him and invited him to sit in the easy chair as I settled onto the couch. I unwrapped the package to find noise-canceling headphones.

Dad looked shy. "I read they're good for HSPs. You said that you're affected by noise."

"Dad, I love them. This is a great present. I've always wanted some."

He got up, reached into his pants pocket, and passed me a miniature tennis ball. "For the cats. I wasn't sure how old they are and if they still play."

"Oh, yes. They do. They're only three. They get bored easily so it's nice to have a variety of toys. Thank you."

Sugar and Flour sprinted into the room as though they were aware a present had entered the picture. I threw the ball, which was heavier than it looked, down the hallway. Flour tore under the couch. Sugar galloped after the ball, batting and chasing it.

"I guess we know who will claim that present," I said. Then, feeling badly for Flour, I knelt on the floor and waved the shoelace at her until she came out from under the couch. Sugar ran back into the room pawing at the ball. I sat on the couch, and Flour jumped onto my lap to watch her sister's shenanigans. Meanwhile, Dad looked amused by the whole episode.

I'd ordered a veggie pizza, which arrived a few minutes later. Despite my protests, Dad pulled out his wallet and paid the delivery guy, giving him a nice tip.

We tucked into the pizza at the dining room table. Sugar took a shine to Dad and hopped into his lap after abandoning the tennis ball. He patted her gently and scratched under her chin.

Dad loved Tristan's painting, and I promised to tell him so.

"I especially like the merry-go-round," Dad said, looking over at the painting above the fireplace.

True to form, I had to regale him with the facts I'd collected about Oceanville Playworld. He agreed it was a neat thought that we were at that moment eating in what used to be an amusement park. This segued into reminiscences of our family trips to Disneyland. We both had a particular fondness for the Pirates of the Caribbean ride.

After dinner, I took Dad on a tour of the cottage, including the back patio. I told him about Sugar's skill at catching lizards and Flour's lack thereof. Then I led him out front, across the driveway, and down the planked walkway that led to the coastal path.

"This is truly beautiful," Dad said as he looked out to the ocean. "Florida is nice, of course, but there's something special about the California coast." We stood still for a moment, watching the waves come in. A breeze ruffled our hair, but it wasn't unpleasant.

"Yes. I'm lucky to live here."

Dad turned to me and touched my cheek. "I'm glad you're happy. It's all I've ever wanted for you."

"Likewise."

We strolled for a bit and returned to the cottage for dessert.

I gave the cats a few spoonfuls of their wet food, then dished up cherry meringue tarts for the humans. I'd frozen a few of my test cases before I left for Valentine's Day weekend and had defrosted them prior to Dad's arrival.

"Just as good as at the hotel," Dad said after taking a bite. "Without the murder."

"Hopefully, that's the last time the tarts, or anything else I make, will be linked with a tragedy like that."

"You can say that again," Dad said. "What's Flour doing over there?" He pointed to Sugar, who was scratching the floor near the food bowls.

"That's Sugar. I know they look similar, but Sugar has green eyes and Flour has golden. I can tell them apart even if I can't see their faces, though it took me a month or so after I adopted Flour to be able to do that."

"They do look alike," Dad said. "Is Sugar trying to convey that she doesn't like the food selection? Is she trying to bury it?"

"No. That's what I thought at first. But what she's doing is hiding the leftovers from predators. So they don't know where she lives."

"That's amazing."

"She doesn't do it all the time, though. And Flour doesn't do it at all."

Dad nodded. "They're very attractive animals. And interesting too."

"Thank you. Is that a weird thing to say? As though I'm responsible for how wonderful they are?"

Dad chuckled.

"I'm pretty crazy about them," I said.

"I can understand that. Maybe I should look into having a cat."

"I think you'd be pleased. Cats have a reputation for being standoffish. I've never found it to be true."

My phone chimed from the couch with an email alert. I went over to get the phone and brought it back to the table.

Christie had sent me a link, which I clicked on. I was taken to a cooking demo on LiveandLearn that Hugo had posted. This must be one of the videos I'd never looked at. I started the demo and held my phone out so Dad could see. In the video, Hugo wore a neatly ironed white chef's jacket and his cowlick was smoothed down. He expertly cracked eggs with one hand and separated them. He proceeded to make a souffle, explaining his actions in a well-thought-out and clear manner.

"Christie sent this. What do you think, Dad?"

"It's interesting . . . and surprising."

"This doesn't track at all," I said. "Sure, he's a good cook, as we know from his hand pies. But remember how he dropped two of them? He's awkward and he trips. He has a teenage vocabulary. He's . . . not like this. Shoot. I should have looked at these demos before. I didn't think they'd lead anywhere."

"Did Christie make any comments?"

I looked at the email. Christie had written:

Hugo didn't come off this way at the hotel. Frankly, I had him pegged as a bumbling idiot.

That was for sure.

"Honey, when you first met Hugo, was it the Hugo we thought we knew or this Hugo?" Dad asked.

I thought back. "I don't know. We didn't have much conversation before the murder. There was the bickering for a while but then we all got in the cooking groove. What are you saying?"

"If he's the killer, he may have assumed the identity of a clumsy naïf to throw suspicion off himself."

"I think you might be right. When the power went out, did he take the opportunity to get back at Edward for firing him?"

"Could be."

"We should tell Detective Hernandez."

"Are you up for going to see him again tomorrow?"

"I don't have much on my schedule. Sure."

I thanked Dad for the presents, he thanked me for dinner even though he'd paid, and we agreed to be in touch the next morning. After cleaning up and getting ready for bed, I stumbled into the bedroom and fell asleep quickly.

THE NEXT DAY, DAD AND I RETURNED to Det. Hernandez's office. I told the detective I had a new theory.

"What happened to the last theory? With Brenda and the pie crust?" he asked. "I thought you had it solved. All wrapped up with a neat little bow."

"Well, I was wrong about that," I acknowledged.

"Hmm," was his only comment.

"Show him the video," Dad said. I started Hugo's LiveandLearn demo and gave the phone to the detective. He watched for a few seconds.

"What am I looking at here?" he asked.

"This is not at all the way he's been acting since Edward was killed. Ask the officer who interviewed him. I think his name was Sykes. I bet he'll agree that Hugo was naïve and awkward. Don't you remember him tripping?"

Det. Hernandez shrugged. "People can be socially graceless yet competent at their jobs. Besides, this could have been done in several takes until he got it right. I don't find anything unusual about it. Probably one of my officers has looked at this already."

I cut my eyes to Dad. "Hugo is the killer, I'm sure of it. He put on an act after the murder so you wouldn't suspect him. I really think I'm right."

"And I think you're wrong. Keep in touch, won't you?"

OUTSIDE THE BUILDING, I SAID TO DAD, "Who exactly does Detective Hernandez think the killer *is*? He doesn't believe it's Brenda or Hugo."

"That only leaves Christie and yourself. He appears to be going with the romantic relationship angle." Before I could object, he added, "Not that you had a relationship with Edward or even wanted one."

I thought for a minute. "How about paying a visit to Hugo tomorrow morning? Since the detective likely won't do it?"

"I'm game."

I PICKED DAD UP AT THE HOTEL the next morning, and we laughed when we realized our blue rain jackets were almost identical. The weather had turned cool and a cloud cover was making things damp. We were thinking along the same lines when we picked our outerwear.

The porch swing was empty at Hugo's house in Greenbrook. For the first time, I wondered if he had seen us coming the last time and run out to the swing, all part of his "gee, shucks" charade.

When he answered the door, he was more Hugo of the demo clip than the Hugo we'd met here before. He wore a blazer over a Henley shirt, and his cowlick was tamed down.

Dad had suggested we be outside with him in case he grew belligerent. Perhaps we had safety in numbers, but we didn't want to take any chances.

"Hey, Hugo," I said. "We're back. Can you come outside to talk?"

"Sure."

We sat on the porch swing.

"What can I do you for?" he asked, pushing his legs back and forth to activate the swing.

"You can cut the country bumpkin routine," I said. "We know you've been putting on an act to throw suspicion off yourself."

He pumped the swing once more before answering. "Okay, yes, it's true I played myself down. I was afraid the police would arrest me because of my link to Edward. He really did fire me. I didn't lie about that. They may have thought I killed him as payback. But I didn't."

"Why should we believe you now?" Dad asked.

"Because it's the truth."

"It would be normal to feel angry at Edward when you saw him again. When the lights went out, you could have taken the opportunity to get back at him," I said.

"Water under the bridge. I have a new job now."

"Which you claimed you're trying to get away from," Dad said.

"I don't know what to tell you. I didn't kill him. Like I said before."

"Do you have any new thoughts on who might have killed him, then?" I asked.

"Did you ever talk to Christie? There was an incident with poultry scissors."

"We already know about that. I asked her," I said. "She said it was nothing."

"Really? That's what she said? Be right back."

He went inside for a moment and came back with a tablet. He made a few keystrokes and showed us a video. "Check this out. A waiter at my restaurant told me about it."

"Who took it?" I asked.

"The dishwasher, I think."

We watched. Christie stood in a kitchen, holding poultry scissors and looking off screen. Edward came into the frame. Thrusting the scissors at him, she screamed, "I'm gonna kill you! I'm gonna cut you up into little pieces!"

Whoa. "Could you email this link to me?" I asked Hugo.

He agreed and I gave him my email address.

"Thanks, Hugo," I said. "We'll look into it."

Dad and I left. Hugo hadn't gifted us with hand pies this time, so we found a café in town and ordered coffee and scones.

"About Hugo," I said when we had our food and drinks in front of us at a window table. "I'm beginning to have my doubts again. Yes, he misrepresented himself, in order that he wouldn't be a strong suspect." I took a sip of my decaf vanilla latte. "But I don't think that means he actually killed Edward. Christie, however . . ."

"Yes. What Hugo showed us was incriminating," Dad said.

"Christie said the poultry scissors incident was nothing. Clearly, it was more than nothing."

"What's your idea for a next step?" Dad asked.

"I think we need to talk to Christie again. Do you have time after we're done here?"

"I'm all yours. Let's do it."

We drove back to Los Robles to the fast-food place. We ordered a cookie in the drive-through since we'd just eaten and weren't hungry. Once again, Christie handed over the order and agreed to come out to the parking lot soon.

Dad and I got out of the car and waited. A few raindrops fell on our heads, so we put up our hoods. We passed the cookie back and forth, and I thought how odd life was. A year ago, even a month ago, I never would have guessed I'd be sharing a cookie with my father in the parking lot of a fast-food restaurant and solving a murder with him. I thought the last time I got involved in a murder was, well, the last time.

When Christie came over to us, I introduced her to Dad and we told her what we'd learned from the video of her and Edward.

There was a long pause. Finally, she said, "I heard about that video. It doesn't show the whole interaction. I put down the scissors and hugged him and apologized. He forgave me. I never would have hurt him. I loved him. Honestly, I wasn't over him by the time I saw him at the hotel."

"What?" I said. "You told me you didn't have feelings for him anymore."

"I lied."

"You seem to have lied about a lot of things," Dad said. "You don't look like you love him in the clip."

"I know. But I swear it's not the whole thing. You know what they say. There's a fine line between love and hate. The true encounter showed both. But love at the end."

"For someone who loved him, you didn't appear very heartbroken over his death," I said.

"I was devastated on the inside," she said. "I still am. I was hoping no one would find out we'd been involved so I was trying to stay cool. Look, I'm not lying now. I didn't hurt him. Honest to god." She glanced at her watch. "I've gotta go. I said I'd be back in a few minutes."

We watched after her as she scurried back to work.

IN THE CAR, I TURNED THE WIPERS ON HIGH as huge raindrops hit the windshield. I said, "I think I better confirm the part about her putting down the poultry scissors and hugging Edward." I pulled over and used my phone to look up the number for Balsamic. I dialed and asked to speak to Heidi, who allowed that yes, perhaps Christie and Edward *had* hugged afterward. I thanked her and hung up, thinking it would have been helpful if she had mentioned that earlier.

I told Dad, "I don't think it matters, though. Christie clearly had strong feelings for Edward, plenty of them bad, if she threatened him like that."

"I agree."

"Dad, Detective Hernandez must have seen this video, don't you think? I don't want to show him something he's already looked at. He'll lay into me the way he does."

"I don't know. This was on a public video channel, right?"

"It was, yes."

Hugo had emailed the link as promised. We looked at the video again and checked the description: *Chef threatens boyfriend with poultry scissors!* Christie's name didn't appear anywhere.

"I don't think it would come up in an internet search," I said. "I didn't find it when I searched for her."

"Detective Hernandez might not have seen it, then," Dad said. "Should we show it to him?"

"I think we have to."

Det. Hernandez said when we walked in, "Oh, goodie. Here you are again. Maybe we should have tea and scones. Do you prefer Earl Grey or English Breakfast?"

Frowning at him, I showed him the video. I detected a slight, but noticeable, lifting of his eyebrows. At last, I'd gotten a reaction from him.

I said, "In the interests of full disclosure, Christie says that after this, she put down the scissors and hugged him. I verified it with one of her co-workers." I looked at Dad. "But this is the smoking gun, don't you think? She actually threatened to kill him."

"We'll keep it in mind," Det. Hernandez said.

He got up to dismiss us, but at least he thanked us as we walked out the door.

As Dad stopped to tie his shoelace on the way out, I said, "Do you think we've done it? Have we solved the case? Is Christie the one?"

He shook his head. "Hard to know, honey. We've thought we were right before."

"I just remembered something Conrad told us. He said Christie's restaurant closed because of bad reviews."

"Yes, he did. What are you thinking?"

"Well, Heidi said Edward and Christie would be acting lovey-dovey one minute and hurting each other the next. What if Edward planted those reviews to sabotage Christie's restaurant?"

Dad nodded. "Maybe. She'd certainly be mad about that. Doesn't mean she's guilty, though. She says she didn't do it."

I sighed. "Do you ever think life would be a lot easier if people couldn't lie? Crimes would be solved more easily."

Dad considered that. "Ah, but sometimes lies are necessary, especially white lies."

"You're right," I said, thinking of the fibs I'd told to Vincent about his baking.

We got into the car and drove back to Oceanville. I dropped Dad off at his hotel and left for home, delighting in the rain hitting the roof of the mini-van. I loved the sound.

Late that evening, my cell phone pinged with an email. I hoped it wasn't yet another cancellation. But this wasn't a cancellation. It was a threat.

You need to butt out of the murder investigation. Mind your own business.

My heart stopped. Who was it from? The sender was identified as *aninterestedparty* with the email address *aninterestedparty@ hotmail.com*. He or she obviously knew how to block their true name from popping up.

I took a minute to decide what to do. First, I replied to the email with the words "WHO IS THIS?" doubting I'd hear back. Then I found Det. Hernandez's card and looked up his email address. I forwarded the threat with a brief comment asking if the sender could be traced.

Trembling a little, I went around the house securing doors and windows and turning on my alarm. I fell into a fitful sleep.

THE NEXT MORNING, I RECEIVED A TEXT from Det. Hernandez saying the email sender had used a VPN and the origin of the message was unknown. The text was brusque and I wondered if he thought I'd sent the email to myself. I called Dad.

"Do you have any thoughts on who *did* send the email?" Dad asked.

"It's either the murderer or one of our suspects who doesn't like being questioned. I'm learning toward the former. Conrad would be the obvious person because of his computer background, but I don't see a motive now that I know Edward wasn't his son."

"I agree," Dad said. "I didn't uncover anything else that would suggest Conrad could be the killer."

"The last people we talked to before I received the email were Hugo and Christie. It could have been one of them."

"Right. But if so, we don't know which."

"This is frustrating work, isn't it?"

"You can say that again," Dad said. "Maybe we need a day off. Care to show me around this town of yours?"

"Great idea."

"Pick you up in half an hour?"

"Sounds good."

FIRST, I TOOK DAD TO THE AQUARIUM. He especially liked the jelly fish exhibit, thinking the creatures quite artistic. We stopped by the special penguin enclosure, where I told him about the cake I'd experimented with a couple of months before. I'd found a penguin-shaped pan online and made half the cake vanilla and the other half chocolate. When I posted a picture on my website, orders poured in and I'd made the dessert several times since.

Once we'd had our fill of ocean life, we ate lunch in the restaurant. Dad refused to have fish, even though the restaurant had won awards for its seafood. He explained that after seeing the many varieties of sea creatures, he couldn't bring himself to eat one of their relatives. I ordered the sole. I didn't have the same compunctions.

We went mini-golfing next. As a seasoned golfer, Dad beat me handily. On one hole, I hit my ball into a water hazard and got wet retrieving it. We enjoyed the ocean-themed course, especially the huge whale where I took seven tries to get my ball through the mouth.

We had coffee afterward at the Otter Café in downtown Oceanville.

"I don't think golf is going to be my sport," I said. "I feel like Flour and her lack of success at catching lizards."

After coffee, we spent some time at the beach and then went out for a casual dinner.

I invited Dad in when we got back to my cottage. We visited with the cats and found an Agatha Christie film on TV. We settled in to watch with a plate of sugar cookies. Dad looked cold, so I covered him with my weighted blanket.

"I should get going," Dad said a couple of hours later. I'd yawned about twenty times by then, so he must have realized it was time to say good-night.

When we'd come in after dinner, we'd thrown our outerwear onto the dining room table. Dad put on my blue jacket, then comically looked puzzled when it didn't fit.

"Why is this so tight? Did I have that much to eat today?" he said.

I giggled. "That one's mine. Here's yours. They really do look alike, don't they?"

Then I froze.

"What is it, honey?" Dad asked.

"Dad, what if Edward wasn't the intended victim?"

"What makes you say that?"

"Conrad was wearing a black blazer on the night of the murder. All the chefs were wearing black chef's jackets. Oh! And Conrad put on a chef's hat to help out with dinner service. Edward had the same build as Conrad and was approximately the same height. We were moving all over the place in the kitchen. When the lights went out, maybe the killer thought he was stabbing Conrad, but it was really Edward."

Dad's mouth opened in an "O."

"What do you think?" I asked.

"If true, we should be looking at who had a motive to kill Conrad. Any thoughts?"

"Not off the top of my head. Oh, wow. This has turned everything upside down. Again."

"Let's sleep on it," Dad said. He gave me a kiss on the cheek and left.

IN BED THAT NIGHT, I THOUGHT EVERYTHING OVER and in the process couldn't fall asleep even though I was dead tired. Could it be true that Conrad was the intended victim?

I decided sleep wasn't coming anytime soon and got up. I found my logic grid and used my cupcake-shaped eraser to delete most of what I'd entered. Fortunately, I'd filled it in with pencil rather than pen. Then I redid it with the idea of Conrad as the victim.

Why would someone kill Conrad? The obvious motive was money since he had plenty of it. I wondered what happened to the hotel and his estate if he died. Would his wife inherit? Or one of his adult children? I shook my head. I wasn't thinking straight. That couldn't be the motive. Neither his wife nor any of his children was in the kitchen at the time of Edward's murder. The only people who could have done it were the same people I'd been looking at all along, and they weren't related to Conrad in any way.

I started with Brenda. Why would she kill her boss? If he died, she potentially could lose her job. If she didn't like her job, she could quit. It didn't make sense.

As for Hugo, he'd been trying to impress Conrad so he'd get the soon-to-be-available full-time chef position. Christie, too, had wanted the job. They wouldn't have a motive to kill him, then. That would have been shooting themselves in the foot.

Although . . . what if Conrad had told one or both they weren't getting the job and I wasn't privy to the conversation? I'd already come to the conclusion that with all the noise and activity in the kitchen, a private word between two of the people present wasn't out of the question. I would have to ask Conrad in the morning. Yawning, I went back to bed.

THE NEXT MORNING, I SLEPT LATER THAN I INTENDED TO because of the sleepless night. It was nearly ten by the time I called Conrad. I sat at the dining room table and sipped on a cup of decaf.

"Did you have a conversation with Christie or Hugo about the full-time job?" I asked him after we'd exchanged greetings.

"The full-time job?" he repeated.

"They were each trying to win you over to get the permanent chef's job that's about to open up."

"I haven't even thought of that since before the murder. No, we definitely never discussed that."

So much for that theory. That only left Brenda. I thought about how to phrase my next question and came up with, "How do you and Brenda get along?"

He didn't answer right away. Then he said, "That's an odd question."

"I know. But I promise I have a reason."

"I'd say we get along fine. I gave her a raise the day before Valentine's Day weekend and she seemed happy about it."

"When you hired her for the open manager's position, that's the first time you'd ever met her?"

"That's right."

"One last question. You'd never met Hugo or Christie before Valentine's weekend, is that correct?"

"No, I hadn't. Kayla, what is this all about?"

"I'm not sure yet. I'll let you know. Thanks, Conrad."

I hung up. I felt like I was going nowhere . . . fast. What was I missing?

I reviewed what I knew about Conrad. He'd founded his successful software company in 1982 and rapidly amassed his fortune. But he'd always loved hotels, so when The Countryside went up for sale, he stepped down as CEO of his company, bought the hotel, and poured his money, time, and energy into the new endeavor. Could one of my suspects have had a vested interest in the hotel under the previous ownership and been upset that Conrad bought it? A vested interest that Conrad knew nothing about? It was a longshot, but I thought I'd better find out. I needed to look for links between The Countryside Inn and my suspects.

I went to the couch, covered myself with the weighted blanket, and did some research on my laptop. As I already knew, the hotel had suffered through earthquakes, a fire, and near bankruptcy. By the time Conrad bought The Countryside and took over, the hotel was barely hanging on.

The previous owner, Bernie Engelbreit, had run the hotel for forty years, taking over from his father, Brighton. I wondered if Bernie was still alive. I searched his name and found he'd died shortly after the sale of the hotel.

Next, I searched for each of the suspects' names along with The Countryside Inn. Nothing came up, other than a few articles about the murder, including one published in the Ocean County Tribune by Toni LaValle that included the quote I'd given her. None of the articles was especially helpful but I was happy to see that Toni had quoted me correctly. I twirled my birthstone ring around on my finger. What to do now?

I remembered the wall of photos in the meeting room where Det. Hernandez had first questioned me after the murder. They depicted the hotel's history, decade by decade. Maybe I'd see one of the suspects in a picture and everything would come together.

Though I wanted to go right away to have a thorough look at the photos, I had a number of orders to fulfill and was starting late.

I texted Dad to tell him I was swamped but I'd talk to him soon. Shutting myself in the kitchen, I spent the next number of hours baking and decorating, then went out in the mini-van to make deliveries. I didn't get back to the cottage until nearly six.

The next morning, I considered cancelling a long-scheduled dental appointment. But I'd already put it off for too long, so I went. The dentist was delayed by an emergency and I had to wait for over two hours. The appointment finally over, I came back home with my gums stinging.

I called Dad after lunch. When he didn't answer, I left a message telling him my plan and I set out for The Countryside Inn.

CHAPTER 14

A T THE COUNTRYSIDE, I PARKED and approached the entrance, taking a moment to drink in the beauty of the venerable inn. Was the hotel hiding the secret to Edward's murder?

Unbidden and completely unrelated to Edward's death, a fantasy of myself coming to the inn during its heyday popped up in my consciousness. In my imagination, Jason took my hand and led me inside the hotel. I pictured us dancing cheek-to-cheek in the ballroom, me in a flapper dress and a jeweled headband holding my hair back, Jason looking dashing in a white suit. Would we be married if we'd met back then? Probably. It was not an unpleasant thought and I filed it away.

I went through the lobby and stepped into the meeting room where I'd been questioned by Det. Hernandez the day after Edward's murder. I turned to the pictures and looked carefully at each one. Stars such as Marion Davies, Claudette Colbert, and Fred Astaire were shown arriving at the hotel, sitting in the lobby, and walking the grounds. Clark Gable and Carole Lombard played tennis on the courts that had since been razed. Shots of the dining room were uncannily similar to what it looked like on Valentine's Day weekend.

The photos traced The Countryside's history in chronological order. Servicemen showed up a lot in the '40s, poodle-skirted women in the '50s. The '60s were all about mini-skirts and long hair. I moved through the '70s and onward to the turn of the century. I examined the most recent pictures extra carefully, hoping something would jump out at me.

Although the photos were interesting to look at, they didn't help me and I certainly didn't see any of my suspects. I started walking away, but something pulled me back. The picture of a cook posing in the kitchen, smoothing down the front of her hair, had drawn my attention. Judging by its placement on the wall, I guessed the photo was taken around the time the hotel changed hands in 2015.

I found Conrad at the front desk speaking to the clerk and asked if he had time to answer a question about one of the photos. He agreed and we returned to the wall.

"Do you know who this is?" I asked, pointing to the picture of the cook.

"I think the names are on the back." He took apart the frame and removed the photo, then turned it over.

"Tabitha. Tabitha Knudsen," he said.

The name did nothing to help me understand why the photo had grabbed my attention. "Do you know what happened to her?"

Conrad looked uncomfortable. "We needed to lay off the staff when we began the remodel. They got nice severance packages, though."

Hmm. Interesting. I thanked him and left.

IN THE CAR BEFORE TURNING ON THE IGNITION, I searched for Tabitha Knudsen on my phone. It took a while, but once I'd followed one lead after another, I found what I was looking for. Tabitha Knudsen, the cook in the photograph, was Hugo Xavier's mother. What I'd recognized was the cowlick, in the same spot as Hugo's. And there was my link.

I was sure I had the basics correct this time, though I didn't have it all worked out. Tabitha had been let go by Conrad when he purchased the hotel. Her son, Hugo, applied for a guest chef position, giving himself a chance to get to Conrad. Thinking he was killing the hotelier in retaliation for his mother's firing, Hugo stabbed Edward by mistake. I put aside the two puzzles of Hugo not knowing the power would go out and why he'd waited so many years to make his move. After all, Conrad had bought the hotel and laid off the workers seven years earlier.

I reviewed my options. There was no use going to see Det. Hernandez. He wouldn't consider yet another theory. I tried Dad once more and didn't get him. Jason? Also no good. Things with him were fragile at best, and he hadn't approved of my continuing to investigate on my own. I would talk to Hugo by myself, but I'd be smart about it.

Deciding my idea to talk to people while in public was sound, I settled on going to see Hugo at the restaurant where he worked.

I knew from the radio story and from Conrad that Hugo worked at a restaurant in Greenbrook, but if I'd heard the name, I didn't remember. A call to Conrad gained me the information that it was a Tex-Mex restaurant called Mesa.

"Do you think Hugo did it?" Conrad asked.

"Yes, I do."

"Why him?"

I hesitated. I wasn't sure I should tell Conrad over the phone that he was the intended murder victim. It required some finesse and I didn't have time at the moment to get it right. Promising him I would explain everything later, I got directions on my phone and turned on the ignition.

As I drove to Greenbrook, I thought over my next steps. If everything went according to plan, I would get a confession from Hugo, which I'd record on my phone inside my jacket pocket. I'd transmit the recording to Det. Hernandez and persuade him to come to Mesa to arrest Hugo. I could only hope that Hugo wouldn't escape before the detective arrived. It wasn't the greatest plan, especially given Det. Hernandez's distrust for me—maybe he'd think I'd doctored the recording—but I didn't have a lot of choices.

The wind picked up and rocked my mini-van back and forth. A few branches broke off trees as I drove into Greenbrook city limits, some landing scarily close to my car. The noise of the wind plus my anxiety about talking to Hugo combined to make me feel aggravated. I told myself to persevere. This would all be over soon and I could go back to my real life of baking, walking on the beach, and dating Jason.

When I arrived at Mesa, I circled the lot and found a space. I switched my phone to airplane mode and turned on the voice recorder, placed the device securely in my jacket pocket, and went inside.

Music blared over the restaurant's speakers. It seemed busy for a Tuesday night, but remembering the date was March fifteenth, I guessed that people were out celebrating payday. Bad for my tendency to get overstimulated and perhaps for the voice recorder, but good for my safety.

I received a look of irritation from the hostess when I approached. She was reviewing the seating chart and had a phone in the crook of her neck. When she hung up, I asked to speak to Hugo and she nodded and left. Hugo came out a minute later, wearing a kerchief across his forehead to keep sweat from his eyes.

"Hey, Hugo," I said, as loudly as I could manage over the noise. "Can I talk to you for a second?"

"What did you say?"

"Can I talk to you?"

He grabbed my hand. "Come with me."

"Wait," I said. But we were already moving. He had a strong grip on my hand and I couldn't break free.

He led me into an empty private dining room, let go of me, and stood in front of the door, essentially blocking the way out. I cursed myself for not being smarter. It was pointless to scream. No one would hear me. It was so loud that if I didn't fear for my life, I'd be cowering on the floor covering my ears. I had two problems now; not only was the voice recorder not likely to pick up our conversation because of the ambient noise, but I was potentially in serious danger.

I looked Hugo over. He didn't seem particularly threatening, and unless he had a gun—or a knife—stowed away on his person somewhere, he didn't have a weapon. Maybe I could salvage the situation. Without giving myself away, I familiarized myself with the room by glancing around. A fire extinguisher was on my right. There was an emergency door at the back, but Hugo could probably catch me if I ran in that direction.

"So, what is this about?" Hugo said, not unpleasantly.

"I think you're the killer," I said, straightening myself up to my full height to back up my words.

"I'm not. I had no motive. I hated Edward's stupid restaurant anyway, so I didn't care that he fired me."

I realized I'd never asked. "Why *did* he fire you?"

He shrugged. "He said I had an 'attitude problem.' Ironic, isn't it? Since he had the hugest attitude there is."

He sounded sincere, but he'd lied before. I was so sure I knew the truth now. And it had nothing to do with Edward firing him.

"I know more now," I said, pressing ahead. "You thought you were stabbing Conrad, not Edward. It was payback for Conrad laying off your mom, who was working at The Countryside as a cook. She was let go when he bought the hotel. That's what happened, right?"

Now he looked annoyed and glanced away. "No."

"Then why?"

"I didn't kill anyone." But his shaky voice gave him away. He was lying.

"I think you did," I said, my own voice quaking.

He closed his eyes and ran his left hand down his face.

"Bernie Engelbreit, the previous owner of The Countryside, died shortly after the sale," he said. "It was a blow to my mother."

Now we were getting somewhere. "Why was it a blow? Did your mother have an affair with Bernie?"

"No! He was old. But they *were* close. Her dad—my grandfather—died when she was a child. Bernie was like a father to her. When Conrad bought the hotel, it killed Bernie, literally.

He had nothing left to live for. It was a double loss for my mother. She lost her good friend and her job all within weeks. She was severely depressed afterward. She was never the same. She couldn't work. My stepdad left her—both of us—and she's been struggling financially ever since. I've had to take up the slack."

We stared at each other. There it was.

"You blamed Conrad for all of that," I said. "So you tried to kill him. Except you killed Edward by mistake."

"I didn't mean to kill Edward. I went over to him—you saw me, didn't you? I wanted to save him, I did. But I think he was dead already . . ." The enormity of what had happened appeared to strike Hugo in full force. He bent over, grasping his knees and panting. Could I make a break for it? Did I have time to get to the emergency exit in the back?

"You have to believe me," he said, straightening up. "All I wanted was to get a full-time job at The Countryside. I wanted to impress Conrad enough so that he'd hire me on. There would have been a poetic justice to that. He fired my mom but then hired me. I'd have the opportunity to talk to him, *really* talk to him. I wanted him to KNOW the ramifications of his actions. You can't just throw your money around and lay off a bunch of good people who need jobs."

I weighed my options. Despite the distress he was experiencing, he probably could still outrun me if I took off for the back door. Meanwhile, he hadn't moved away from his position of blocking the door we'd come through. Would I be able to distract him enough so I could escape?

Hugo went on, "Conrad was so careless about Bernie, not giving a damn that The Countryside meant everything to him. Bernie put his life savings into the hotel. He was even living in one of the suites because he'd lost his house. Conrad offered him so much cash he couldn't refuse. So Bernie had money but not what he loved."

I let that all sink in. "Okay, but what happened to your plan? Why did you try to kill Conrad even before the event was over and you hadn't talked to him about the job?"

"Because he was so full of himself, so happy about the event. You heard him. Going on and on about how wonderful it was. How great it was going to be for business. I got madder and madder, thinking about what he'd done to Bernie and my mother. When the power went out, I snapped. And then it wasn't Conrad I stabbed. I felt awful about it."

"I believe you," I said.

He looked me up and down and a tremor ran through me.

"I can't go to jail," he said. "You see that, right? I have to support my mother. She needs me."

"But you have to, Hugo. You have to go to the police and confess."

"I don't. You're the only person who's worked it out. You should have minded your own business and butted out."

His phrasing sounded familiar. "Wait. Did you send me a threatening email?"

"You were like a dog with a bone. I could tell you weren't going to give up. I tried to warn you, but you didn't listen." He advanced toward me, his hands reaching for my shoulders.

And then the wind howled and the lights went out.

CHAPTER 15

I DARTED OVER TO WHERE I REMEMBERED the fire extinguisher was on the wall. My instincts were right and I lifted it away. I needed a couple of tries but managed to pull the pin and aim the nozzle in the general direction of Hugo's face, hearing him sputter and scream at me in response. I dropped the extinguisher and sprinted toward the back door, its "EXIT" light thankfully working in the dark.

Out on the sidewalk, I looked both ways, trying to get my bearings in the pitch blackness. I went the wrong way before realizing the parking lot was in the opposite direction. I spun around, dodging a branch that came flying at my face. The wind was making an insane amount of noise. As I neared the parking lot, the wind died down for a second and I picked up the sound of shoes slapping on the sidewalk. I let out a strangled cry. Hugo was after me!

"Kayla! Is that you? It's me, Dad."

I stopped running and turned around. I could barely make out my father's silhouette.

"Careful, Dad," I warned. "Hugo's the murderer. He was going to kill me."

"It's okay, honey. Detective Hernandez got him. He can't hurt you now."

I sank to the ground, overwhelmed with relief. "How did you... how did you know I'd be here?"

"I got your message and was worried you might get into danger being on your own. I tried calling you but I couldn't get through. I got in touch with Conrad to find out if you'd been at the inn. He said you'd decided Hugo was the killer and you'd gone to Mesa to talk to him. I called Detective Hernandez and asked him to meet me here."

"You convinced him?"

Dad nodded and gave me a hand to help me up. "I told him I was quite certain you were in danger and he believed me. The hostess said you'd gone into a private dining room with Hugo. I knew you wouldn't do that voluntarily. Detective Hernandez and two officers went inside, guns blazing. They found Hugo doubled over, coughing. He confessed and went with them willingly."

"Thank god."

"K-Bear, you caught the killer. Well done." He gave me a timid smile and we hugged. In a wonderfully symbolic gesture, the streetlights came on just at that second.

DAD DIDN'T WANT TO LET ME OUT OF HIS SIGHT, so once I'd debriefed with Detective Hernandez, we asked the owner, Arturo, if it was all right to leave my mini-van in the lot overnight. Arturo said the car could stay as long as I liked, and he thanked me for my part in apprehending Hugo.

"I never liked the guy," he said. "He's a good cook but there was something off about him. I'm glad he's gone."

When we were settled in our seats in the rental car, Dad laid his blue rain jacket across my lap.

"Take good care of that," he said. "The blue jackets led to your correct and ingenious idea that Conrad was the intended victim." He handed me a bottle of water and I took a long sip. When he seemed satisfied I was okay, he turned on the ignition.

He drove us in the direction of Oceanville, swerving around branches scattered across the road. The wind had finally stopped.

After a while, Dad said, "K-Bear, I can't tell you how happy I am that you're all right. But I feel we might have some unfinished business. I've been reading that book you told me about, *The Highly Sensitive Person*. I read this morning that HSPs are deeply affected by troubled childhoods."

"Yes, I remember that."

"I'm sincerely sorry for how I handled the times when you were overstimulated."

"I know you are, Dad."

"I've never told you much about my own childhood," he said. "Did you ever wonder why?"

"I guess not. I'm sorry. I should have."

"It's all right. I didn't like to talk about it. My father was very strict. We didn't have much of a relationship at all. So, when you were young, I didn't have any experience with being a loving father. This isn't an excuse, just an explanation. I got punished. I thought it was what parents did. Now I know it's damaging. Particularly to you as an HSP."

A tear ran down my cheek. I felt sad about my father's childhood and sad about my own. At the same time, I was moved by his words. "Dad, I wouldn't say my childhood was bad. There were good times. Like The Pirates of the Caribbean at Disneyland. And The Christie Project."

"I'm glad to hear that. I want to have a closer relationship with you. I think we're off to a good start. I want it to continue."

"I want that too."

"Good. I think, despite the murder, our seeing each other again has been a great success. Do you agree?"

"I definitely agree."

A big smile made its way across his face. "On that note, may I take you to a celebratory lunch tomorrow?"

"I'd like that."

AT HOME, I TEXTED ISABELLA to let her know what had happened. I needed to tell Jason too, but how? I'd put myself in danger despite his warnings and he wouldn't be happy. I turned on the news to see if the media had gotten hold of the story yet. Hugo's arrest was mentioned, but not my name, so I had a brief reprieve.

I took some quiet time to deal with all the feelings the day had stirred up. First, there was what happened with Hugo. Adrenaline had kept me from collapsing into a slobbering mess while the confrontation was going on, but now I trembled, remembering the peril I'd placed myself in. Would Hugo have killed me? Probably. He'd killed before.

As if the face-off with Hugo wasn't enough, there was the conversation with Dad in the car. That had turned out in the best possible way, but it had been intense and a strain on my already overstimulated system.

What I really wanted to do was talk everything over with Jason. I went to bed to get some rest, hoping my dreams would give me clarity on how best to approach him.

DAD AND I RETRIEVED MY CAR from Mesa the next morning, then caravanned to the wharf. I thought about taking him to Fishes Do Come True but decided against it. I had to make things right with Jason first. We went to Sam's instead.

Out on the deck, we basked in a mild sun with no wind in sight.

I broached the subject of my quandary over Jason. "I don't know what to do, Dad. He's going to be mad that I didn't take his advice and stay out of the murder investigation. He was right. I put myself in danger."

"He's worried about you. It's natural."

"I know."

Dad waited a beat and said, "K-Bear, based on what you've told me, I believe Jason is a good man. I don't want you to lose him. You can work it out, can't you?"

I took this in. "I think I know exactly what I have to do. I've known all along, but something was holding me back. If I've learned nothing else from these last few weeks, it's that life is short. I'm ready now."

We spoke of other things after that: Art in all its different forms, nature, and food. It was fun to realize that Dad and I had similar tastes. We liked the same kind of art and music, and preferred the same cuisines.

At the end of the meal, we walked to our cars in the wharf parking lot.

Dad said, "I'm going to book a flight home tomorrow morning. It's time to get back, work things out with Stacy, and start my new life."

"Okay." I felt myself choke up. "I'll miss you."

"It's only so long, not good-bye. We'll be in constant touch."

"Yes. Thank you for everything."

"Thank *you*, honey."

I wanted to say something to him that I hadn't said since I was a little girl. "I love you, Dad."

He looked surprised and pleased. "I love you too, sweetheart. So much."

We hugged. I waited until he got into the car, turned on the ignition, and drove off. I kept watching long after he was gone.

LATE THAT AFTERNOON, I RESTED ON THE COUCH, glancing at my phone every few seconds. Should I call Jason? No, what I needed to do had to be done in person. As I started to get up, the cats got to me and crowded themselves onto my lap. So much for that plan.

There was a knock at the door a few minutes later. The cats refused to hop down and climbed onto my shoulders. We moved as one entity to the door.

I found Jason on the step. A red sweater, which looked familiar, was over his arm.

"Hi," I said.

"Hi. I miss you."

"I miss you too. I was about to come down to the restaurant to see you."

"Can we talk?" he asked.

"Sure. Let me just detach my pets from my body." I bent down and Flour and Sugar jumped to the floor. Jason and I settled onto the couch.

"Oh, this is yours. You left it that day at the restaurant," he said, handing over the sweater.

"Right. Thanks."

Then he reached into his pocket and came up with what looked suspiciously like a ring box.

"Jason . . ."

"Just open it."

Inside was a pin shaped like a merry-go-round, and if I wasn't mistaken, the *Playworld* merry-go-round. I couldn't believe it.

"Where did you get this? How did you know?" I asked.

"Isabella told me you'd been researching Playworld and that you were excited about it. I found this at the history museum gift shop."

It was one of the most thoughtful presents I'd ever received. Jason was a master at choosing the perfect gift.

"Thank you. I love it." I put on the red sweater and positioned the pin on my chest.

"It looks good. Happy belated Valentine's Day."

"Right back at you. I have something for you too. It's also from the museum."

I went to the bedroom to retrieve Jason's gift, which was encased in a long mailing tube. Back on the couch, I laid the tube in Jason's lap. He took the end off and pulled out the poster I'd found at the museum. He spread it out onto the coffee table for a better look.

"This is wonderful," he said. "It's the wharf?"

"Yes. This is how it looked in the nineteen twenties," I said.

"Very neat. Thank you. I'll have it framed and hung at the restaurant." He reached over and kissed me. "Care to go for a walk?"

"I would."

We walked companionably along the coastal trail. Jason took my hand as we strolled.

"How are you?" I asked.

"Aside from missing you? Good. The restaurant's been busier than usual, thanks to the top chowder award."

"That's great. You deserve it. I've always known you made the best chowder."

"Good to hear. Your opinion is the only one that really matters to me."

That made me smile. "Jason, I have to tell you something. You were completely right. I put myself in danger again." I told him about my confrontation with Hugo—being trapped in the private dining room, the lights going out, the fire extinguisher, and how I'd escaped.

He expressed his concern, but nicely didn't say "I told you so."

"Thank god you're all right," he said, stopping to kiss my forehead. A few tears gathered in his eyes and a shiver of guilt ran through me.

We started walking again. "I have to apologize," I said. "I should have taken your opinions and wishes into consideration. You didn't want me to investigate because you thought it was dangerous and I did it anyway. While I'm at it, I'm sorry for not telling you I went to see Leon last December."

"Well, thank you for all of that. But, fortunately, it's unlikely you'll be in a position to investigate a murder ever again."

"Right. Never again."

"Do we need to talk about anything else?" he asked. "Let's get it all out there."

"I overheard you and Craig that night on the deck. He said I wasn't the right girl for you. And . . . you didn't disagree."

"I did indeed disagree. I may have taken some time to gather my thoughts before I spoke, but I definitely set him straight."

"And? How did he take it?"

"He took it well. I told him you're an introverted HSP and can be unnerved by certain social interactions. I explained about the murder and said how stressful things have been for you. I made sure he understood that you're smart and capable and kind and creative, and the best thing that's ever happened to me."

I took a few seconds to absorb that. "Wow. That's really nice. I feel the same way about you."

"He'd like to have dinner again if you're up for it."

"Yes. Second time's the charm. I'm sure I'll be more articulate."

"I'll arrange it."

There was more to cover. I had to say the words I'd been unable to express for too long.

I took a deep breath and put my hand to his arm. We stopped walking.

"What is it, honey? Is there something else?"

I collected my thoughts and spoke. "I admit I've been scared. The last time I said this, well, it didn't work out so well. But I had no idea what I was doing back then. I do now. Not because of a quiz or because I'm trying to keep up with someone else's relationship or any other reason outside of me."

"Should I be following any of this?" he said with a grin.

"What I'm trying to say is . . . I love you, Jason. I love you very much."

He took my face in his hands and kissed me four times: on my forehead, each cheek, and then my mouth—for a delightfully long while.

"It's about time," he said when we pulled apart.

"You were waiting?"

"Yes, I was waiting. And I love you too."

In contrast to the first time he'd told me he loved me, I felt a pleasurable tingle start at the top of my head and make its way down my body.

"Those have to be the best words in the English language," I said. "Other than 'let's go eat.' Which I think we should do right now, by the way."

Jason threw back his head and laughed, and like a pair of lovers in an old movie, we walked into the sunset.

THE NEXT MORNING, I REALIZED I had another baking lesson scheduled with Vincent. Today we were making cheesecakes. For the first time since I'd begun teaching him, I felt a heavy sense of dread at the prospect. None of his assignments had worked out so far and I was beginning to wonder if any would. After delaying for as long as I could, I trudged down to the restaurant.

Isabella saw me enter the lobby and came over.

She gave me a hug. "I'm so glad you're okay."

"Thanks, Iz."

"Would you like some coffee?"

I shook my head. "Baking lesson with Vincent."

"Well, don't look so excited about it," she teased.

"I confess I'm feeling resistant. Every lesson so far has been an abject failure."

"It's nice of you to keep persisting," she said.

I nodded, though I wasn't convinced I was doing Vincent or myself any favors. I told her good-bye and went into the kitchen for the next disaster . . . er, lesson.

This time, we almost set the entire kitchen on fire. Fortunately, Vincent was able to quickly put out the flames with the extinguisher, the patrons in the dining room being none the wiser.

In the quiet that followed the near calamity, I asked softly, "Vincent, why is baking so important to you?"

He ran a hand across his bald head and didn't meet my eyes. "My mother died when I was seven."

I touched his arm. "I didn't know that. I'm sorry."

"She baked all the time. I would help by handing her tools and ingredients. Sometimes I'd be allowed to mix the ingredients and lick the bowl. Each time we baked, she'd tell me a story about the dish: how she'd had it as a little girl, or out with her sorority sisters in college, or with my father in a restaurant. I learned so much about her life when we were baking. Those are my strongest and most treasured memories of her."

"And by baking now, you're remembering her."

"Yes."

I wanted to be as sensitive to Vincent's feelings as possible. "I don't think baking is your thing, Vincent. No judgment. It's just how it is. There are plenty of things I can't do. Like run a restaurant, which you do incredibly well." I smiled.

"I know you're right. I'm hopeless at baking," Vincent said. "But it's hard to hear. I really wanted a way to honor my mother. I still miss her so much."

"I bet there's something else you could do to keep your mother in your heart," I said.

"Like what?"

"Well, what kinds of things did the two of you do together besides bake? Do you remember anything?"

He thought for a moment. "There was a merry-go-round we visited in Los Robles. We went almost every weekend. She always rode one of the horses. I preferred the lion. I liked it because it was the only one and so regal."

"Good. I'm going to think about that. There might be something there."

"Thanks for caring, Kayla."

I HEARD FROM CONRAD THE NEXT DAY. Detective Hernandez had given him the lowdown on Hugo's arrest. Conrad thanked me for my part in solving the murder.

"I think the hotel will survive now that Hugo's been apprehended," Conrad said. "Although . . . bookings were already picking up. Maybe the murder has added a layer of mystery to the hotel that people are relating to."

I wasn't sure if that was interesting or ghoulish. "I'm glad."

"I've decided to stop the guest chef weekends," he said. "But I'm going to add a special dish to the regular restaurant menu and name it after Edward. I'm leaning toward chili since he won his first award making that."

"Great idea."

Conrad hesitated for a second and then said, "I want you to know that I've taken to heart what happened to Hugo's mother and the other staff we laid off. First of all, I'm going to offer Tabitha the open chef's position. Then I'm going to start using my money for good. I'll be sponsoring scholarships and making it known in the community that I can be approached to fund projects."

"Conrad, that's terrific. Really."

"This has been a wake-up call for me," he continued. "It's humbling to know that Hugo wanted to kill me for my poor choices. I feel like I have a second chance."

"I'm happy I was able to help."

"I owe you, Kayla," he said, choking up. "Anytime you want to come to the hotel, I'll comp it. Stay as long as you like. I'll give you our best suite. Just let me know."

"I will. Thank you."

I hung up, thinking that Jason and I might finally have our romantic getaway.

I'D PROMISED VINCENT I'D FIND ANOTHER WAY for him to honor his mother. But what? I put my thinking cap on later that night. A solution presented itself while I was deep in sleep. I dreamed that Jason and I were hanging out at Oceanville Playworld at the carousel, which featured cats instead of horses. Jason and I rode a large calico with a long tail. When we got off, all the cats came alive. Jason and I laughed and laughed, and I woke up with a smile on my face. What a neat merry-go-round that would be. More importantly, the dream was the key to what I wanted to do for Vincent.

I drove to The Countryside to see Conrad after breakfast. I asked him for what I needed, and he agreed readily, saying it was exactly the kind of project he was interested in funding. Next, I stopped by the Seaside Shores offices and told Miranda my thoughts. She said it would have to come before the board of directors but she had a feeling they would agree as they'd already been discussing something similar.

Satisfied so far with how my idea was being received, I went to see Tristan on the way home. He showed me a few of his new art pieces, which I did my best to compliment. As often happened, I found them unique but not to my taste. I asked if he'd be willing to participate in my grand plan. In response, he grabbed me and gave me a big bear hug. I took that as a yes.

I RETURNED TO SEE VINCENT THE NEXT MORNING. Isabella told me he was in the kitchen, so I went in. He looked to be doing inventory and made a note on a pad before turning to me.

"I've got it," I said. "A way to honor your mother."

"Already? That's great. What's the idea?"

"Conrad Cunningham is funding the construction of a merry-go-round in Alden Park. What do you think of running it for two hours a day, between lunch and dinner? You wouldn't get paid, but it could be valuable in other ways."

"That sounds incredible."

"I think it will be a wonderful way to remember your mother. Plus, you'll be making a lot of families happy."

Vincent nodded slowly. "Yes. This is perfect. Thank you very much."

"You're very welcome."

I started to leave but he called me back.

"I have to place another order for desserts," he said. "I'm officially hanging up my apron and rolling pin."

I grinned.

DAD AND I DECIDED TO HAVE a VIDEO CONFERENCE every week to catch up. We tried it for the first time a few days later. After we chatted for a bit, Dad held up an Impressionistic painting of The Countryside Inn that made me gasp.

"You painted that?" I asked.

"Yep."

"It's fantastic, Dad. It's really, really good."

He laughed. "There are a few flaws but thanks for saying. Stacy and I are doing fine now. I hope you can get to know her someday. But, in the meantime, I have a new lady for you to meet."

"What? Dad, I don't know . . ."

He disappeared for a moment and came back holding a darling tiger cat.

"Oh, my gosh," I said. "How adorable."

"This is Miss Marple."

"I love her," I said. "Hi, honey."

"She's three, just like your cats. I got her one of those tennis ball toys. She bats it around and chases it through the condo. Sometimes she goes out to the patio to sun herself. She hasn't caught any lizards, though. Which is okay by me."

"I'm so happy for you."

"Me too. Talk soon, honey."

"Bye, Dad."

THE NEXT DAY, I WENT INTO THE KITCHEN TO BAKE. The night before, I'd dug around in the freezer and come up with whipping cream and raspberries, which I'd put into the fridge to thaw.

I made up vanilla cake batter, tinted it pink, and baked a batch of cupcakes. When they were cool, I sliced off the tops. I whipped my thawed cream and folded in the raspberries. Next, I spread raspberry jam on the bottoms of the cupcakes, added generous amounts of cream, and put the tops back on. I sifted powdered sugar onto the cakes and affixed small fondant hearts. I carefully arranged the finished cupcakes in one of my light blue bakery boxes.

After putting the cupcakes in the fridge temporarily, I baked and frosted a few dozen spring-themed sugar cookies; flowers, rabbits, and chicks. When they were done, I stored most of them and wrapped up the rest. I got ready to go and went outside to the mini-van.

I drove over to the house where my late friend, Trudy, had lived. When the new resident, Lois Jeong, answered the door, I introduced myself and she invited me in.

It was difficult being inside my friend's home without her there, but Lois had very different tastes than Trudy. It didn't seem like Trudy's house anymore, which made me feel somewhat better.

Lois and I ate a few of the spring-themed cookies. When I got up to go, a golden retriever ambled into the room. Lois introduced him as Rollie. I rubbed his ears and promised to visit again soon.

Next, I drove to La Tierra to Melody's house. Once again, she was outside in the backyard and I went through the gate.

Melody greeted me fondly, exclaimed over the raspberry cupcakes I'd brought, and gave me a hug.

"The detective called to tell me the killer has been apprehended," she said. "I saw it on the news as well. I knew you wouldn't have hurt Edward."

"Thank you for believing in me," I said. "I'm glad Hugo has been taken into custody. I hope it helps a little knowing that your son's murderer has been caught."

"It does." She looked back at me thoughtfully. "It was a shock to find out Edward wasn't the intended victim. But it's comforting as well. The idea that someone hated him enough to kill him had been weighing on me."

I told her I understood and we said good-bye.

I TOOLED BACK TO THE COTTAGE, THINKING that everything was wrapping up in the best ways possible. As an added bonus, Christie called soon after I got home, her voice raised in excitement.

"I got a new job," she said. "I'm going to be head chef at a restaurant in Santa Cruz. It's called Forks and Spoons. I've rented a bungalow near the beach. I hope you'll come and see me some day."

"I will. Congratulations, Christie. I'm really happy for you."

Just as I hung up, the phone rang again. Isabella.

"Channel 444," she said.

"What? Hello to you too."

"Turn on Channel 444. The local Oceanville channel. Now. I'll talk to you later."

Muttering to myself over Isabella's bossiness, I did what she said. I turned on the TV and sat on the couch. I switched the channel to 444, wondering what to expect. A commercial was on. So? But then I realized what was happening. The commercial was about *me*.

I couldn't believe it. Client after client came on to sing my praises; not just about my baking ability but about my character too: Vicky, Eileen, Jan, Vincent, and then Isabella and Jason. After Jason, Angie appeared. She was on the walking trail, halfway between the community and the wharf.

"Kayla is really, really nice," she said. "And she makes the absolute best desserts." She was distracted by something to her left where the ocean was—probably an otter—and ran out of the frame. I smiled. She was so cute.

A blown-up picture of my business logo, with my phone number and email address highlighted, ended the ad. Tears poured down my cheeks. I felt very much like George Bailey in *It's a Wonderful Life*. I had the best friends and boyfriend in the world.

FEELING EXHILARATED OVER HOW WELL EVERYTHING was turning out, I sang "Wild Thing" to the cats as I fed them their wet food later.

I lifted up Sugar's paws to dance with her, but she objected with a loud meow. I let her go back to eating.

I danced into the living room and sang some more. The hairs on my neck stood up and I whipped my head around to the window. The window, which I'd flung open to catch the ocean breeze, was filled up with someone's face. Detective Hernandez? What the heck? I opened the front door.

"What are you doing here?" I asked.

"Nice song," he said. "May I speak with you?"

My face ablaze with heat, I gestured to him to come in.

"Would you like some cookies?" I asked, wondering why in the world I was being so polite to him.

"Sure, that would be nice."

"Why don't you sit in the chair? I'll be right back."

"Don't let me keep you from finishing your song and dance routine."

"That's okay. I'll be only a minute."

Flour and Sugar, now done with dinner, were washing themselves on the living room floor, unperturbed that we had a visitor. Before sitting down, the detective went over to them and gave them a few gentle pats. I begrudgingly gave him credit for being kind to animals.

I went into the kitchen to make up a plate of sugar cookies, then returned to the living room.

"These are pretty," Det. Hernandez said as he looked over the pink rabbits and yellow chicks. He removed a chick from the plate and lowered himself into the easy chair.

I thanked him, chose a rabbit, and placed the plate on the coffee table. The detective took a huge bite of the chick, almost decimating the entire cookie at once.

"Quite good," he said. "You're talented. At baking. Not necessarily singing and dancing, but definitely baking."

"Thanks."

"You're welcome."

"Okay, Detective. This is very nice and all, but why are you really here?"

He finished the cookie in another bite, brushed crumbs from his fingers, and said, "This isn't something I normally do, but I'm here to apologize."

"Apologize?"

"I wasn't fair to you. You solved the case and I'm grateful. I wanted to wish you well."

"I wish you well too."

He stood. "I should let you get back to . . . whatever. Good-bye, Kayla."

He went out the door, leaving me flummoxed that he'd called me by my first name and that we'd reached a détente.

"What do you think about that?" I asked the animals. Then I realized Sugar was alone in the room and the front door was ajar. I was so surprised by Det. Hernandez's visit that I'd left it open the entire time.

A few seconds later, Flour came in the front door and dumped a lizard at my feet.

EPILOGUE

Ten weeks later, I was thrilled to find a flier and invitation from Conrad Cunningham in the mail. The flier announced that The Countryside Inn would now be offering decade-themed events six times a year. First up, a 1920s weekend in two weeks. The dining room would serve Roaring Twenties food, and the grand ballroom would host a *Great Gatsby* dinner dance on Saturday night.

Conrad had written a personal note to invite me and a guest to the weekend, everything gratis.

"Woo, hoo!" I now had the perfect plan for Jason's and my first getaway.

I called him.

"Hey," he said. "I was just thinking about you. And the hand pies you served for dinner last night. You more than the hand pies."

This kind of greeting was much improved from our "stilted" period.

"I put the fruit pies onto my website for ordering," I said. "I think I finally got them to the point I want them to be. But I have something else to talk to you about. Something very interesting." I told him all about the 1920s-themed weekend.

"I'm in," Jason said. "I'll get out my Gatsby costume and leave Timothy in charge."

"You have a Gatsby costume?"

"No. But I would really like to rent one."

"Then I shall be Daisy to your Gatsby." We talked for a few more minutes, arranged to have dinner in downtown Oceanville, and said good-bye.

When I called Isabella to tell her about the weekend, she abruptly hung up on me. She didn't call back for twenty minutes.

"Sorry," she said when I answered the phone.

"What happened?" I asked. "Did Vincent walk in?"

"No, no," she said. "I'm not at work. I'm going later. I wanted to call Brian and then phone the hotel. We're going to the nineteen twenties weekend too!"

"That's awesome, Iz. We'll have so much fun. A double date."

"Clear your schedule. We're going to the costume store tomorrow for our twenties garb."

I agreed.

BEFORE I LEFT FOR THE 1920S-THEMED WEEKEND two weeks later, I stopped by the new merry-go-round at Alden Park, timing my visit for when I knew Vincent would be there.

Conrad had provided old pictures of Playworld's carousel to the builders and asked them to adhere to the original design as much as possible. They'd done a wonderful job, supplemented by Tristan's painting of the horses. He, too, had stuck to the original design, but in true Tristan fashion, also included his own special touches. Each horse had a different-colored saddle and reins, and he'd painted a shell on each pony's right cheek. They were beautiful.

Vincent saw me and called me over.

"Hey, Kayla, what do you think? Business is booming."

"I think it's great. You seem really happy."

"I am. I know it's probably fanciful thinking, but I feel my mother here with me."

"Maybe not entirely fanciful." I smiled.

"I've been thinking. I believe it's possible she went to Oceanville Playworld as a child," he said, keeping an eye on the riders as the carousel turned. "She lived in Los Robles when she was growing up. She could have visited Playworld in the late nineteen forties. I don't remember her mentioning it, but it could have happened."

"I bet she did visit. It's my understanding that families came from all over the county."

"I don't know how to thank you. First of all, for the baking lessons, and then for arranging all of this."

"My pleasure, Vincent," I said. "I'll see you soon, okay?" I touched his hand and went home to get ready for the weekend.

ISABELLA ARRIVED AT MY COTTAGE an hour later, just when I was putting on lipstick. I said good-bye to the cats, happy that Vicky and Angie had agreed to come visit them twice a day.

Isabella and I went outside to wait for our ride.

Jason and Brian had gone in together and rented a period car for the weekend. The two drove up to Isabella and me as we sat in my Adirondack chairs on the porch. Brian, who was driving, honked the horn, and we giggled at the noise, which sounded like a duck in distress. Jason, next to Brian, waved.

"How are you, my choice piece of calico?" Jason asked as he got out and directed me to climb into the backseat. He followed me in and patted my knee.

"Um. What?" I said.

"In the nineteen twenties, it meant a desirable woman. I thought you would appreciate the calico reference."

I laughed. "I do. You know me so well."

"And how are you, Bearcat?" Brian said to Isabella when she slipped in next to him in the front.

"What did you just call me?"

"It's a good thing," Brian said. "It means you're spirited and lively."

"Oh, okay. That's all right, then."

"What do you think of the car?" Jason asked.

"It's really neat," I said, and Isabella nodded in agreement.

Brian huffed. "It's not 'neat.' This is the coolest car ever. It's a Model T. Do you feel these leather seats? See the brass details?"

"Just tell me it's not going to break down on the way," Isabella said. "That's all I care about."

"No way," Jason said.

We drove to the hotel, taking back roads because of our low speed, talking and laughing the whole time. The parking lot at The Countryside was crammed full of cars, including some other period vehicles. The hotel looked happy to once more be in its element, gleaming in the late afternoon sun. I remembered my fantasy of coming to the hotel in the 1920s with Jason, and I felt I was actually living it. He took my hand as we went inside.

Conrad was greeting each guest at the door and appeared happy to see me. He gave me a kiss on each cheek. I introduced Jason, Brian, and Isabella, and they each shook hands with Conrad.

"Enjoy yourselves," Conrad said. "I'll see you at dinner." He directed us to the front desk to get our keys.

Jason and I settled into our room. Conrad had given us a huge suite, so we had a bedroom, living room with fireplace, and even a balcony. We chatted and read our books outside.

At five-thirty, we began getting ready for dinner. I took a long bath in the luxurious tub with lots of bubbles. Jason brought me a root beer and I sipped on it as I bathed. Sheer heaven. An hour later, we met up with Brian and Isabella outside their room on the floor below ours, and the four of us went down to the dining room. We were served Waldorf Salad, Chicken a la King, and pineapple upside down cake for dessert. I wasn't too fond of the latter and decided not to try my hand at it anytime soon.

After dinner, the four of us took a walk around the grounds, and I told everyone where the tennis courts and pool once stood. We repaired to our respective rooms, and Jason and I had a relaxing— and romantic—night.

In the morning, we ate pancakes, a popular breakfast food in the 1920s. We were also offered codfish cakes—which I declined— and grapefruit. Isabella tried the codfish cakes and said they were delicious.

We watched a documentary about the hotel and went on another walk. After we'd eaten lunch and played a few board games, it was time to get ready for the big dinner dance.

I put on my flapper dress and headband while Jason donned his white suit. We went downstairs to the ballroom, holding hands.

Dancing with Jason cheek to cheek—just like in my fantasy—I didn't think I had ever been happier. A lot of people loved me and appreciated my work. My dad and I had come to an understanding about my childhood and now had a strong relationship. My family and friends were healthy and happy. I'd had some stressful times lately, but all of that was behind me. Life was good. Life was *great*. And it promised to go on that way for a long time. What could possibly go wrong?

THE END

CAROL AYER, A HIGHLY SENSITIVE PERSON (HSP), lives halfway between San Francisco and Sacramento with her cat, Rainn. When she's not writing, she's reading mysteries and thrillers or watching movies and cooking shows. As a native Californian, she visits the ocean as often as possible.

www.carolayer.com